All the strong minds...who at some point gave up!!

YOU ARE NOT YOUR MENTAL HEALTH

A COLLECTION OF SHORT STORIES BY WETALK WRITERS ON MENTAL HEALTH

WETALK WRITERS

Contents

Disclaimer

Acknowledgements

Stories are not just a product of a writer's passion and hard work, rather, they are undisputable teamwork by people surrounding them trying in their best possible way to render support while the writer bleeds with pen and paper. We acknowledge all the support extended and thank them from the bottom of our hearts!

- *"I would love to thank my dear friend Hema Nair who has always been a constant source of support and motivation for my writing. I would wholeheartedly thank my maashi, Dr Anuradha Chackroborty for painstakingly reading and reviewing my stories repeatedly correcting mistakes, especially from a doctor's perspective. I am very grateful to WeTalk for giving me the opportunity to write and have my stories published."* - **Author Saswati Sinha**

- *I wanted to express my heartfelt gratitude for the opportunity to publish my story through WeTalk. I am truly grateful to Hema Nair for recommending my name and to the entire WeTalk team for believing in my work. Thank you for this incredible opportunity.*- **Author Arun P T**

- *I am profoundly grateful to Tara for her incredible bravery in sharing her mental health journey with me. The way your nature became open has not only enriched this work but has also provided hope and inspiration to countless women who may be facing similar challenges in hormonal imbalance like PCOD. I would say your story is a testament to the resilience and strength of the human spirit and I am honored to have the privilege of telling it. Thank you for trusting me with your experience shared and allowing me to bring your story to a wider audience.-* **Author Tanushree Dholpuria**

- *An opportunity to be a writer is rare, and to top it off, I have been blessed to have people in my life who inspire me. I'm grateful to the constant pillars of my support as well as criticism, my family, whose opinions envisage my own. I also have my soul sister to thank, Saswati Sinha Mishra, for linking me to this wonderful program, led by Sheeba and Vinay Kulkarni. And above all, I thank my Ma, who is, has, and will be forevermore the Northern Star to my sails.-* **Author Sudeshna Das Chakravarty**

- *It was indeed the toughest of tasks to weave a story around mental health. I take this opportunity to thank my eldest daughter Anamika, who stood by me reading and rereading the draft and correcting me whenever and everywhere possible. She would say- Mom, you better not write a suicide note. It looks more like a motivational note!-* **Author Sheeba Vinay**

- *The credit and thanks for this story goes to my better half Sheeba Vinay, for creating a literary platform (WeTalk Writers and Literary Agency) motivating and instilling the confidence in me to restart writing and write to make a difference. To our kids (biological and furballs) for being a strong and moral support to me during my writing process.-* **Author Vinay Kulkarni**

Quotes From Authors

"*Feel free to open up your fear and get help so that you knowingly or unknowingly don't pass Intergenerational Trauma to the next generation -* **Lakshmy (Author of The Recurrence)**"

"*Open up your heart to listen, so that the one in pain can speak. -* **Saswati Sinha (Author of The Pink Affair & The First Born)**"

"*I have known that the only way, to get back from the brink of losing yourself is to give time and gather yourself up, piece by piece; day by day. One day at a time. This is the best way but the toughest way. -* **Vinay Kulkarni (Author of One More Round)**"

Foreword

The arena of mental health has experienced an exponential shift, not just globally but also in Asian and South East Asian countries. In India, as well, there is a gradual movement in how we have approached the topic of mental wellness. Unlike physical health, mental health space has lot of ambiguity, right from locating mind in the human body.

However, no one can refute the impact our moods and feelings have on our appetite, sleep, work performance, relationships, and beyond. Yet for lot of our folks mental health is still not a priority. A common misconception around mental health could possibly provide a rationale for these trends; mental illness and wellbeing aren't the opposite of each other, and so lack of mental disorder doesn't necessarily ascertain living a healthy life always. While referring to mental health, a three-way approach can be helpful: Preventive- identifying the present mental state and building mental muscles for resilience, Supportive - acknowledging and validating a need to seek professional help, and transformative - enhancing existing state of wellness.

This paradigm further emphasises the need to seek support and therapy from a professional as a means to maintain one's state of wellbeing as well, and not limit it to eradicating clinical disorders. In fact, this threefold

approach taps into the power of sharing narratives; when we share are lived wisdom with others, as a community we heal, evolve and grow. With time, as professionals, we have also learned the social elements responsible for developing and maintaining disorders on one hand, and healing and supporting during distress on the other hand. And this realisation gets validated in a collectivistic culture as ours. Hence, the onus of mental health and wellbeing of an individual is also determined by their larger tribe, and each one of us is a contributing force of this ecosystem.

Dr. Shambhavi Samir Alve
Ph.D. Psychology, MBA - HR, CMT-P
Co-Founder, EmptyMyndscape LLP
Psychotherapist
Alternative Healing practitioner
Certified Mindfulness Coach - Professional (CMTP-065)
Vice-President, WICCI's National Mental Health Council
(NMHC)

Introduction

"It is a sad plight that very few have the privilege and access to mental health care even though mental health can be effectively treated and at a relatively low cost." - Sheeba Vinay

You Are Not Your Mental Health is a phrase inspired by one of the articles I was reading for my syllabus reference. It struck me hard. How true can it be? How well could we probably understand that?

Mental health is one of the most important topics discussed across the world. On a recent account more than 14.3% of deaths worldwide, or approximately 8 million deaths each year, are attributed to mental disorders. Studies reveal that this number is only going to increase in times to come. Mental health disorder comes with no gender disparity or age difference. Right from children to elderly persons are affected by mental health issues each passing day.

However, when it comes to talking about or acknowledging mental health issues it is still considered as a taboo and a topic of societal stigma. In our country where the majority are a young population, it is alarming to see the sudden spike in issues related to mental health. We can attribute this to various factors- Unhealthy lifestyle, digital addiction, peer pressure, etc. However, we are deprived from an adequate understanding of the topic, resulting in neglecting the importance of mental health. The most amusing part about it is that even the educated crowd is ignorant when it comes to their mental health.

Most of us are unaware that mental health is our legal right too. The right of a person with mental health conditions to food, water, personal hygiene, sanitation, and recreation is an extension of the right to life as in **Article 21** of the Indian Constitution.

Under **Section 18** of the Mental Healthcare Act 2017, equal access has been granted to all individuals irrespective of their culture, caste, class, etc. Making mental health not only your human right but also your legal right. Hence denying or neglecting the mental health of a person is denying the legal rights of a person.

The month of May is considered Mental Health Awareness Month. Worldwide campaigns are held to create awareness of the importance of prioritizing our mental health. We, at WeTalk Writers unapologetically believe in keeping our mental health sound. And "You Are Not Your Mental Health " is a collection of short stories by us. Our little contribution towards the cause.

In the end, we do believe that it is mandatory to recognize that a sane mind and healthy thinking is a contributing factor to the overall healthy physical well-being of a person. Unarguably!

- **Sheeba Vinay**

CHAPTER ONE

A Part of Me, You Never Knew

Harsh dialed Amin's number once again.

He is still not picking up the bloody call. Why does he always do this? Harsh now started to lose his patience. I had convinced Sweta, to get ready at this hour of the day just to cater to his bloody whims.

It was Amin's idea to go for an early morning trek. He was badgering Harsh for a long time. Even though, Harsh enjoyed outdoor activities with Amin, owing to Sweta's third trimester and related complications, he avoided staying out for a long time. He had even opted for a WFH option to stay close to her. However, Harsh was bad at saying no when it came to Amin. And here he has been waiting for him for the last two hours.

Harsh and Amin were childhood friends. "Two peas in a pod" kind of friendship. Harsh grew up to be a jovial person, with a flourishing career and a sturdy settled life. While Amin grew up wild, untamed and reckless. He switched jobs overnight. Fought with parents over silly matter and almost gave up on his love life with Faheba. The only factor both the childhood friend had in common was their unconditional love for each other. No matter what, they had their back when the world stood against them. Many a times.

Amin was dealing with a lot, lately. He had recently left the job that didn't go well with his parents or Faheba. Arguments and wrangles became an everyday routine at Amin's place. Faheba on the other hand had already given him an ultimatum and now the relationship had hit rock bottom. Slowly he was beginning to go insane.

Harsh was the only person who stood by him during this tough time, be it dealing with Amin's parents or trying to patch things up between him and Faheba. But now nothing seemed to work!

Some days Amin would sulk in his thoughts, sleep for hours, eat irregularly. But some days he would be a different persona altogether. Full of energy, blasting with enthusiasm to conquer the world, go travelling, pursue hobby and meet new people. And this trekking plan was a part of one such mood swing!

How about a road trip? You and me? Amin asked, out of nowhere.

Road trip? Where? Harsh inquired lazily.

Kerala to Kashmir, a bike trip! Amin looked excited.

Harsh stared at him a murderous look.

Are you nuts Amin? Don't forget Sweta needs me now. I have taken WFH just to be by her side. Harsh soundly visibly irritated.

Amin started sulking. Harsh smiled at him. Let's plan something else. Something nearby. I promise a bike trip before this year ends. I promise!

******

Harsh grew impatient. Amin had called him thrice last night just to confirm about trekking and warned him not to be late. Now he had ghosted him. Harsh decided to go and check on him. The moment Amin's mother opened the door for Harsh, he knew something was out of place.

What happened Umma, did you cry? Harsh looked at Amin's mother doubtfully.

Amin came home late last night, all drunk and was crying uncontrollably- Umma looked concerned. Do you know anything? Harsh nodded. He didn't talk to us, didn't say anything. You talk to him Harsh mone (Son), he only listens to you. Amin's mother was almost in tears.

A stinging smell of alcohol pierced his nostril the moment Harsh entered Amin's room. Amin was in a deep sleep. Harsh decided not to wake him up. It was almost noon when Amin woke up from the sleep. He saw Harsh sitting at the corner of the bed looking at him. Amin broke down, hugged Harsh and sobbed like a child.

Late night, after confirming trekking program with Harsh, Amin opened Faheba's message which he ignored since morning. He stared at the message for quite a long time. It read-

Amin, I am getting married this week. I have waited enough for you, can't betray my parents anymore. Bye Amin. You left me no choice!

****

Amin started plunging into silence. He talked less, drank more. Cried a lot. Harsh couldn't bear the sight of Amin walking into self-destruction. He knew professional help was needed.

Dr. Bhagyashree was a well-known psychologist who Harsh knew personally. She was his colleague's spouse. Even without Amin's permission, Harsh booked an appointment for him. Now the herculean task was to get Amin to agree for a session.

You think I am mad? You think I am a nut crack? Amin raged with anger.

It's okay to be not okay Amin, it's okay to seek help.

Don't throw that philosophical bullshit on me. Keep it to yourself.

For me, once, just this once. I won't ask you again. Harsh pleaded. Amin gave in.

That's when he landed in front of Dr. Bhagyashree that weekend. He sat there uncomfortably and looked around aimlessly.

Amin, how are you feeling today? Doctor smiled at him.

It didn't take more than 15 minutes for Amin to open up. He broke his silence in a more dramatic way. Various emotions poured out of Amin vehemently. He stayed calm while talking about his childhood, emotional while talking about his grandparents. He was enraged remembering his feud with parents and friends. He cried like a child in a single mention of Faheba!

However, the only time he smiled was while talking about Harsh.

Harsh is an all-rounder, he is just the way I would love my life to be. He was a topper in school, whereas I struggled just to clear all my subjects. He was everyone's pet, including my parents, and I was the one who went unnoticed. During our college days, it was all about Harsh. Girls were crazy about his looks and boys were a bit insecure. He topped amidst all the distractions thrown at him. He found his love in Sweta. While I was relegated to just one word- loser!

Amin took a deep breath. Doctor noticed a glint of jealousy. She concluded the session there!

She asked Amin to stay positive and prescribed few affirmations and meditation to keep his mind at bay.

Is that all? No medications or pills? Amin looked surprised.

No, I don't prescribe medicine Amin. Doctor smiled.

Your next session will be on Monday.

****

Harsh was waiting impatiently in the visiting room. He jumped out of the seat at the very sight of Amin coming out.

How did it go?

Such a waste of time- Amin complained, I am not coming back!

Harsh looked exasperated.

******

The very night, Harsh called Dr. Bhagyashree unable to control the curiosity.

It's too soon to say anything Harsh, doctor said. Few more sessions will be required before deciding. Anyways, I doubt your friend will attend further sessions.

Harsh could hear her smile through the phone.

He was silent as he knew she was right. Amin needs a productive phase right now. He needs to deal with the insecurities that he is nurturing. Try to convince him for more sessions if possible. Harsh was apprehensive when the call ended.

He had no idea how to persuade him for next session.

This was not the first time, Harsh had been dealing with Amin regarding visiting a counsellor. Harsh knew Amin had been struggling with his emotions for a long time. Even though people around him had different opinions and prescriptions for his condition-

Get a job son- Parents said

Focus on your career, focus on us- Faheba warned

Get him married- relatives advised

You are a loser- Friends laughed
Fuck everyone- Amin thought!!

But it was Harsh's suggestion that amused Amin to the core that he laughed rolling on the ground. Visit psychologist? Aru nyano? (who me?)

Have you lost it Harsh? He laughed. All we Malayalees need is a chilled beer or maybe two. So, let's go-

Their conversation always ended abruptly.

Harsh, however was not ready to give up on Amin this time. No chance. His frequent mood swings, anger issues, sleeplessness and overeating are not good symptoms. I need to push him for the next session. Harsh thought.

And that's exactly what Amin was thinking.

This bloody sun of a gun will deliberately do anything to make me say yes for the next session. The only way to avoid that is to ghost him for few days. Amin had the habit of ghosting people whenever the situation went against him. He would take a break and leave without telling anyone, not even Harsh. Mostly the ghosting was to avoid Harsh for a few days. He couldn't say no to Harsh, so he would just disappear and then return one fine day as if nothing happened. Sometimes it would go from few days to few months.

Amin desperately wanted to get out of this situation. He could not stand to watch Faheba getting married. Moreover, couldn't handle Harsh and his counselling madness right now. Need a break!

He didn't think twice-

Shoved some clothes into his bag pack, started his bike and rode off without telling a human. He withdrew sufficient funds from the nearest ATM and switched his phone off.

****

Two weeks of utter peacefulness. Solitude. Finding self.

Amin had no idea how fast two weeks passed, in a blink of an eye. He travelled within the boundaries of his state. But visited the less touched places. Where human presence least bothered him. He felt nature at its best. A surreal calmness wrapped him. He had never felt like this before.

His heart still fetched the wound that Faheba gifted, he still missed Harsh. But what tempted him more to return was the aroma-filled small kitchen where his mother cooked. No matter what the situation was, Umma never missed to cook Amin his favorite fish curry mixed with tamarind and more with love. Amin was tempted to relinquish the taste once again. Maybe I should end this madness here. Maybe I should return home - Forever!

At the end of two weeks, Amin returned home. As he was close to his place, he felt few known faces staring at him. Not just staring but looks mixed with despair and agony. Why the hell are they ogling me? Or am I just assuming? As he was closer to his house. He felt a sense of fear creeping him. People had begun to crowd around towards him. Mother! She was not well when I left. Amin's thought started to scare him.

He recklessly parked his bike and ran towards his house. But to his surprise the door was locked. That scared him more. He looked for someone to answer from the small crowd that already gather at his doorstep.

Amin Mone, go to Harsh's house, they are waiting for you there.

Wait why? What happened? Someone from the crowd sobbed, few of them murmured. Amin could not hear anything. He aimlessly ran towards Harsh's house. As soon as he was near the entrance of the house, he knew something was not right.

He had barely entered the house when he saw Sweta lying on the sofa, half awake. She was mumbling in her stupor. Someone noticed Amin standing at the door, and cried out. It not only shocked Amin, but also woke Sweta up with a jerk and she stared straight at Amin.

She slowly walked towards Amin. Walking dead. Amin watched her. A woman with beauty and grace looked nothing but a dead soul.

Where were you? She asked in a tone that scared Amin.

I... even before he could complete the sentence, Sweta slapped his face with all the energy left. Amin went blind for a moment.

You bloody looser. My Harsh always stood with you. And you left him when he needed you the most. Take this and get lost Amin, you dare not show me your face again. Sweta shoved a half scrambled half folded paper in his hands.

Amin looked at the paper for few minutes, his eyes again went dark. His heart refused to accept what his mind already knew.

He opened the paper carefully and slowly as possible.

His heart sank as he read the first line-

My dearest Amin,

A fear crept into Amin's body and his hand started to shiver. He started to read one of the most painful letters he had ever read, he would ever be reading in his lifetime.

My dearest Amin,

Only you, it is only you I am thinking right now, at this moment, when life is willing to give me everything I could possibly ask for, but my mind is not ready to take it further. How I wish for you to be here at this moment. Maybe I will ditch the plan like I had done a hundred times before. Just looking at you. Hearing your rubbish talks. How I wish you were here right now!

There are millions of things I want to tell you through this letter. However, there won't be much time left for that. I am in a hurry. More than my hurry you won't have the patience to read an elongated letter. So, I will keep this as small as possible. But at least hear me out this time. I have a part of me that you never knew!

Amin, do you remember the first time we met? At the school library corridor. We were hardly 7, right? I was hiding from the rest and crying. You handed me a half-eaten popsicle without asking me anything. I ate that without saying anything. Do you know what that half-eaten popsicle did to me? It soothed the pain of a 7-year-old who was violated by his math teacher inside an isolated library room few hours back. The pain still pierces my heart. It went on for 4 more years. I always wanted to tell you, but didn't have the guts. It broke my spirit completely Amin, but you know what hurt me the most? My mother! She told me to stay quiet about the incident as it may harm the family's reputation. I was broken. Yet I continued to fake a smile on my face. I became a good actor.

While growing up I was weighed upon the ambitions of my father more than mine. He wanted me to pursue Engineering and secure a job that would buy material things and family reputation. Nobody asked me what I actually wanted. History, I wanted to pursue history and teach kids!

During college days, I was on the run to secure the position of the topper. I always envied you Amin. You lived a life with no inhibitions, with no fear for future. It was the worst days of my life Amin, when each and everybody around me looked at me as an achiever, I was completely lost, broken on the inside.

It was then it started, a sudden bout of anxiety started crippling me every now and then. It was during the second semester PL; I had my first panic attack. I collapsed in my bedroom. Doctor told my parents that I was dealing with anxiety and stress. My father laughed it off, my mother unable to understand what I am going through, poured her heart into feeding me more food. I didn't say anything, I didn't want to hurt them. You were on your usual disappear mode. I waited for you desperately. But once you returned, I didn't feel like telling you. Your presence was enough!

While dating Sweta, I felt I had overcome the fear, anxiety and the frequent suicidal thoughts that I started to carry by then. I was wrong. By the time we got engaged, I was more or less struggling to cope up with the entire situation. I wanted to tell Sweta everything, and call off the marriage. But didn't have the guts to do that. Soon Sweta became my entire world. She always wanted the best for me. Everything perfect! Can you believe I even turned vegan?

With each passing day, when everything seemed to be normal, I struggled a little more. In silence, my mind dwelt in chaos. However, I tried to survive.

Then something happened.

I met the math teacher at our family temple few months back. He smiled at me, a malicious one. He chatted with my parents, blessed Sweta, showered me with praise. The 7-year-old in me stood hapless again. On the way Sweta had good news, we are soon to be parents. Happiness knew no bounds. Everyone looked at me. I sat, frozen. I was happy yet felt suffocated, my heart started beating fast, I started to panic. I couldn't bring a smile on my face. I tried hard. Sweta was upset with that. Later that night I apologized.

But that started a new chapter in my life. I slowly slipped into a darkness where I found no doors to close or open. I felt alone. I became suicidal. The thought of ending everything crept into me frequently. I was scared. I am more scared now. I have started to hear voices. Someone talking to me in my head.

Asking me to harm everyone. Sweta, my unborn kid, you...

I have no control over me. Amin, hence, I decided to bid adieu, forever

Please tell Sweta that it's not her fault, tell acchan and amma that I am sorry, it's not their fault too!

Amin, I wish you were here now, hear me once. But I guess it's too late.

Sorry for breaking the promise of our bike tour...may be in the next life.

Amin, it is not your fault, nor mine.

My mind is tricking me into doing things-

Amin – keep our memories alive, keep me alive

Live a part for me, that I wish I had lived!

Your friend forever....

Note from the Author: Of late dialogues around mental health have raised drastically. Right from children to the elderly are aware of their mental health rights. Fortunately, or not, this exactly has become a point of concern. People across the globe are behaving as if they know all about mental illness. A bit of laziness, procrastination and we name it "Depression" without even knowing the extremity of the illness called depression.

Don't assume- We never know who is suffering silently, hiding pain behind their smile. All those who call out are not suffering, and all those who are silent may not be doing quite well.

This story is a small message towards it!

Author- Sheeba Vinay

Sheeba Vinay is a literary agent, publishing consultant by profession, a Law student by ambition. Her write-ups have been published in Lokmat Times, TOI and various platforms like Women's Web. Sheeba Vinay is the founder of WeTalk Literary Agency, a writing community and literary agency for budding writers and authors. She has authored a Children's ebook with Storyweaver Pratham Publication. She also has compiled various titles under WeTalk that are available on Amazon and Flipkart!!

Sheeba carries a keen interest in Volunteering activities and is the co-founder of WeTalk Legal Rights advocating GBV and JJ. She is also the president of WICCI Telangana

Women's Laws in India Council, a member of the National Mental Health Council, WICCI and a brand ambassador of Apni Shala, promoting Mental Health awareness among children. She has been V-Force leader (Hyderabad) an initiative by United Nations Volunteers.

CHAPTER TWO

The Pink Affair

Of rivulets and ramblings

Little rivulets of rainwater ran down the glass window relentlessly. Torsha's eyes were fixed hypnotically on those busy little trickles, as if they were on an urgent errand. She pondered, whether most people around her were like those rivulets, meaninglessly running after something throughout their lives. Or did they resemble teardrops of all the souls, who strived to outlive their pain. The soft orange glow of the streetlamps looked mysteriously beautiful through the haze that formed on the pane. The drenched canvas outside resembled a sabotaged painting where all the hues and colours got washed and blended with the rain, ran onto the glistening wet street and into the gutter. With trembling hands, in apprehension and a hint of fear, she picked up the menu card and ordered her favourite sundae, three scoops of strawberry ice-cream, strawberry sauce, jelly, strawberry wafers and cherries on the top: The Pink Affair.

A hundred miles away from home

Once every month, over the weekend, Torsha and Barsha would make sure that their dad took them to Scoop, the ice-cream parlour that hung over the Hooghly River. Enclosed completely within glass panes this quaint little ice-cream shop overlooked the majestic Vidyasagar Setu, across the river on one side and the Calcutta Chakra Rail on the other. The siblings were always consistent in their orders, The Pink Affair. While the order would be prepared, they would keep shifting from one side of the glass covered wall, to another, either to watch a steamer boat on the river or the train chugging on its old tracks, whistling away in the darkness of the evening. Dad meanwhile would sip his coffee and watch his lovely daughters in glee. This was their favourite activity, a ritual done once every month. They called it the Pink Affair Day.

On one such evenings, the siblings happily jumped into the back seat of dad's car, waving their ma goodbye and were soon on the way to the Scoop. Singing, chatting, squabbling, they were almost near their destination... but the fateful moment awaited around the roundabout. A monstrous truck speeded towards them, dad had immediately perceived the break failure of the erratic vehicle and the consequences of it jamming into their car. He quickly positioned his car in such a way that his daughters would be unharmed by the swerving beast of a truck. That evening, none of them had Pink Affair, none of them reached the Scoop.

Home, they brought her warrior dead

Ma waited for dad to be brought home. No words were spoken, not a drop of tear welled up in her eyes. She just sat there stone-still, so was dad, under a white sheet, both motionless, both without any signs of emotions. Barsha, over-enthusiastically tried to attend to the crowd of people, offering them water, being chirpy, as if everything was normal, nothing changed that evening or in their lives. She was in a denial mode, which seemed concerning. Torsha went upstairs to her room, closed the door, switched on the Shiva Stotram and started to dance. It was a dance that would send chills down one's spine. It was a dance so exhaustive that one would feel dizzy watching her. She danced as if her whole being was set on fire and she was rising from it like a phoenix.

Ma suddenly got up, went to Torsha's room, held her by the hair and started beating her up mercilessly, shouting "why did you come home? Why could you not bring him with you? You should not have come back either, not without him!" Torsha did not resist; she had not protested to say there was nothing she could do to change the course of events and situations. She started feeling numb, a swarm of tiny black dots engulfed her, she heard a high-pitched endless beep in her ears which travelled to her head and then she collapsed into darkness. When she had got back her consciousness, she had found herself alone in her room. She perceived, thereon, without dad, it would be an "alone" journey for her. She had always been closer to dad than Barsha. Barsha was more the mommy's girl. It took her some time to realise that, dance would be her only companion for solace. She got back on her feet and round and round she went, her feet, gliding on the marble floor, one hand up in the air, the other pointing at the floor. She twirled and swirled, like an opiated whirling dervish.

She was all of nineteen, when the following morning she saw her dad's body, still covered in a white sheet, slide into the electric furnace, no smoke could be seen rising from in there, navigating their way up in the sky, to form a star. A star which she could perhaps see whenever she looked up at the night sky. That was the last time she would be seeing dad, she thought, feeling void from within. Maybe a cemetery would have been more tangible, to bury dad, he would be there, lying under the soft soil, green grass covering him. She would visit him and talk to him sitting by the fresh flowers she would have taken for him. Maybe, the gods could have stopped them from going to the Scoop that Saturday evening, of 3rd November 2001. Maybe the time could have slowed down, and the entire event of the crash could have been stopped by the press of a pause button. All the thoughts crowded up in her mind. There was no rewind button, nor the pause. She drowned his ashes in the river that flowed silently by the crematorium. She was left with nothing, except for his memories.

Fire in the hearts

Weeks turned into months. No one discussed each other's emotional turmoil at home. No one discussed dad. Each of them carried dad like a fire in their hearts. Each of them tried to feel dad's presence in their own ways, behind the closed doors of their rooms. They could smell dad, they could talk to dad, but all individually, never together. The dynamics of their mental state was totally disrupted and disheveled.

They fought their own lonesome battle, unknowingly distancing themselves from the outside world. None of them attended family gatherings or celebrations. Soon the indifference was reciprocated by the relatives and friends. Their world was seemingly as much haunted as their double storied house. The garden was a chaotic patch of wilderness, the balcony railings had started chipping colours, the once beautiful iron gate, rattled as if it would fall apart under the burden of grief and pain, the paint on the house looked weary and weathered with the passing seasons of life.

Ma waited for dad to come home. Though she had resumed and rejoined her work after 6 months, but she would not go out anywhere else to socialize with relatives, friends or colleagues. She experienced constant anxiety, of losing her loved ones. The fear, that one day her daughters might not come back home, grappled and suffocated her. So much so that, if the siblings were late even by few minutes, she would run to the street carelessly crossing roads and wait at the bus stop. She dreaded that she would have to see them wrapped in white sheets, lying motionless in front of her. She would not want them to go out unless it was absolutely necessary or urgent. She lived every moment of her life in "death anxiety".

Barsha, believed that dad had gone for an official tour and would soon be back home. She was happy in her own little make-believe world. Sometimes when it would seem to her it was too long for an official trip, she would cajole herself into believing, dad is time travelling into space. He was not a star up there in the sky though, she would think, because he would come back one day. She dwelled happily and peacefully in the sanctuary of her imaginary world. She waited for dad to come home. Barely was she aware that she was in complete denial of dad's sudden and unexpected demise. She would not budge from her self-assuring theories of dad's absence and eventual return.

Torsha, had lost control over her thoughts, they were growing like a vicious mycelium in her mind. Sometimes they were like a whirlpool of untamed, unruly eddies with their own current, lipped with foams of whims and fancies. Other times they were like a congregation of elves working without harmony. She could not stand the sight of any father-daughter relationship, be it a billboard advertisement, a kid on the road walking past with her father, her cousins with their fathers, or a group of girls discussing their fathers in the crowded public transport. She just could not tolerate the sight of any father-daughter together or hearing about them thereof. Tears would roll down her cheeks uncontrollably; her mind would scream "WHY ME?! WHY ME?!" A battalion of overwhelming thoughts, with tentacles of hatred, anger, anxiety, anguish, got the better of Torsha with each passing day. She fought hard against them, but they seemed immortal. Every time she tried to cut a tentacle off, it regenerated, regrew to be more monstrously painful for her to handle. She suffered from complicated grief and bereavement disorder. She would have delusions of that fateful night repeatedly, waving goodbye to ma, the speeding truck, the unplugging of the ventilator, dad covered in white sheets, the metal gates of the electric furnace, all would come up alive as if someone was replaying the series of events. Then a long beep, drifting and tugging her into dark emptiness. Leaving a jet-black tarpaulin flapping in the wind.

Where the rain drop had to die

Months turned into years. One day as she was walking past a park Torsha, decided to while her time and listen to some music on the Walkman dad had gifted her on her 19th birthday, the last birthday gift she had received from him. The park benches were all painted white, just like the white sheet dad was covered in, when he was brought home for that one last time. Torsha did not like white anymore, not even Rajnigandhas. But that day she decided to sit a while on the white bench. She chose a bench under the Palash tree, lit a cigarette and drew in a long puff. The smell of cigarette smoke made her feel dad around her. She smoked dad's cigarette brand. It gave her a different high. The smoke from her puff, meandered up towards the reddish-orange bloom. The tree looked like it was on flames, no wonder Palash is called the "flames-of-the-forest", she pondered. The fallen flowers, on the bench looked so bright and alive, radiating more life on the otherwise dead-white benches. Visuals of that fateful evening came flashing in her mind yet again like a high voltage electric shock. Dad lay on the bed in the Intensive Care Unit, his chest heaved high and low, he was breathing, yes! he was, he was alive! Torsha told herself, until a junior doctor came in to unplug the ventilator. Apparently, it was his duty to inform the family members that "he is no more, it's the mechanical ventilator, that's causing the pattern of inhalation and exhalation, that is why it looks he is alive and still breathing..." he went on with what seemed like a cruel heartless blabbering, "now I shall unplug the artificial airway, next I disconnect the breathing circuit, now the gas supply... see now as I unplug the electical supply...." he continued, considering himself a dutiful doctor. Torsha could only hear a deafening beep inside her ears, which travelled to her head. That was the first time she heard the maddening beep. Her vision gradually changing the spectrum of colours : white sheets, splashed with red blood stains, blue overalls, curly fumes of incense sticks, metal furnace, she running to dad, dad on the white bench, flaming red flowers sucking up the cigarette smoke; all the fragmented visions converged into a lump of monochrome. "Didi, didi, pass me the ball please..." came a distant voice, which strangely restricted and prevented her from blacking out, the shroud of jet-black tarpaulin had not covered her.

She opened her eyes to see a little wide-eyed girl, clinging to a rag doll, standing a meter away from her. Torsha, picked up her ball from under the bench, called the little girl to come closer and asked her to sit beside her. They both chatted chirpily, when suddenly Torsha realized there was no adult with the little girl. On enquiring where her parents were, she answered saying "they have become stars, didi, I live in that orphanage!", pointing out to a dilapidated building across the park. "You should not be alone in the park you little cherub", Torsha affectionately chided her and picked her up in her arms and walked towards the orphanage.

Torsha's life took another turn thereon. She never dared to ask her dreadfully selfish question "WHY ME!? WHY ME!? She realized thereafter, how so many kids were either abandoned by their living parents or dead. She gradually tamed all her unruly thoughts and got Ma and Barsha around to visit the orphanage. They named it "Vritti" and opened a trust in dad's name to financially support the kids living there. All three of them rediscovered the presence of dad, by being a loving support to the orphaned kids. Their obsessed mindset of clinging to dad and his memories gradually gave rise to little wings of sanity, better means to cope with their tremendous loss, their mental setbacks and turmoils. A galore of pretty wildflowers bloomed in their otherwise unkempt, chaotic garden. The disarray of tangled overgrowth had the hint of colour and beauty that sprouted amongst them. Their lives seemed like a little green that peeped from under the arid land where it had been waiting for a little drop of rain, to help it sprout with life.

Of rivulets and reflections

She was hesitant and apprehensive about planning the evening at the Scoop, but Ma had insisted. She was expecting Ma and Barsha to arrive anytime. They had asked her to order just one sundae, so that all three could share together. While she waited for her order to be prepared, she looked at her reflection on the glass pane of the ice-cream parlour. It was a pale haze. Mist had gathered on the pane with the warmth inside.

She extended her arm and touched the glass pane, the rivulets of rainwater ceased running. The rain was a light drizzle outside. She drew the outline of a face with her finger on the foggy glass. She smiled contentedly, her reflection quietly falling on the mist-face and overlapping the outline she had sketched. Then she drew two more faces. Smiled again and tilted her head to see them from all angles. Drew a mouth, for each face with parted lips. Torsha then, whispered "Speak misty ladies, speak! Speak your hearts out here on!' That evening ensued into a fresh new chapter of Pink Affair.

CODA

Ma was suffering from what is called "death anxiety" in psychological terms. It is an intense fear of death or the dying process, where one is tremendously anxious about losing any loved one after having suffered the loss of a loved one. In psychology, it can have dire consequences if the anxiety gets out of control. It is also known as "Thanatophobia". Ma dismissed psychological counselling and tried to regulate her own fear and anxiety, accepted death as an inevitable and has learned to move on for her daughters' sake but is looking forward and wishing to be with dad at the soonest possible.

Barsha, was suffering from "denial" or "abnegation", which is a psychological defence mechanism postulated by psychoanalyst Sigmund Freud, in which a person is faced with a fact that is too uncomfortable to accept and rejects it instead, insisting that it is not true despite what may be overwhelming evidence. She graduated as an engineer and works for an MNC with elan and responsibility. She has learned to cope with dad's absence and believes one day she will meet him on the other side of the rainbow bridge.

Torsha, suffered from complex-grief disorder or bereavement disorder, which had plummeted and manifested symptoms like delusions and black-outs. She runs a well-established dance academy and is the mother of a lovely little daughter. The beautiful relationship her daughter shares with her doting dad, Torsha's loving husband, brings immense joy to Torsha. It is probably a delightful reflection of Torsha and her dad that she sees in them. Time did not heal the pain, it has just taught them to live with the pain in a better way.

Author- Saswati Sinha

Saswati Sinha is a mother, educationist, entrepreneur, a child psychologist and holds a PhD in medical microbiology. She has a quirky sense of storytelling which has made her a favourite amongst kids over the last one and half decades. She loves writing anecdotes, diaries, and comic strips. She has authored several scientific articles and research papers. In this anthology, her stories highlight mental health conditions we undergo but often ignore the gravitas of the same. Intending to sensitize one and all to the importance of mental well-being she hopes that her readers will have valuable takeaways from this anthology.

CHAPTER THREE

The Recurrence

"And Mama Bird, Papa Bird and the Baby Bird lived happily ever after."

Vidhya closed the Children's story book and looked at Eesha. She was surprised to see her six-year-old baby doll still awake, fixing her eyes at the ceiling. It's an every night routine that Eesha goes to sleep with a story from her mother. But today she was not able to. Something was troubling her. Vidhya was about to ask her the reason at once the pair of cute little eyes shifted their gaze from the ceiling. Looking straightly at her mother's eyes, the girl asked, "Ma, will Papa love me again as he used to be? Rithu says there are dads who don't like girl children. Is it true?"

Vidhya looked at her aghast. Vivek's avoidance of Eesha was not so vivid that only Vidhya as a mother could identify it. May be its true that children observe things much better than adults, sometimes. But she didn't expect this to affect Eesha this far that she shared the same with her classmate and best friend, Rithu. Hiding her pain, she hugged her daughter, kissed her cheeks and said, "You are the one whom your father loves the most in this world. You are his little princess and his little princess forever."

"Are you sure?"

"Trust me!"

"Good night, Ma"

"Good night my sweety." Vidhya pressed her lips on Eesha's forehead.

The moonlit night, the starry sky, the cool breeze; nothing could fade the fire of pain inside her. Standing at the balcony, clutching her hands around the railings, Vidhya closed her eyes as if revisiting those golden days of her life. She thought herself to be one of those luckiest women in the world; loving parents and in laws, caring partner, charming daughter, a dream house, a profession of her choice. Life was smooth till a few months ago, till Eesha's sixth birthday, to be precise.

Vivek! Even a thought about him made Vidhya realise her pain, her temper fading away. Her memory journeyed back to her high school days. A tall, slender boy with a grim face and police hair cut whom she met for the first time in class 8, Vivek, son of Major Chandrashekhar, was a new student of the year. He and his mother had returned back from his father and got settled in their native place. A brilliant student, sharp and witty but he always showed his uneasiness when pointed out in the group or asked to answer questions orally. He always avoided eye contact. Unlike the other boys of his age, he was never influenced by his peers, always kept a distance from others, that made him a loner in the class; a typical introvert who finds solace in solitude.

It was three months later that the more realistic face of Vivek got revealed when his father was killed in a military operation. We were taken to visit when the body was brought home. There we saw him bold and strong with his arms around his mother who was leaning against him for a support. He was calm and composed more for his age. That maturity was what struck her the most. The care he gave to his mother seemed astounding.

He was always considerate as a son which was evident when he himself initiated his mother's second marriage, years later. Vidhya remembered with a pain how he missed his father even years after. Later after their marriage he used to pour his heart out, crying loudly like a child in her lap thinking about his father. The only one with whom he shared his thoughts, pain, pleasure, doubts and dilemma was Vidhya. They were perfect made for each other couple.

A week after the final rituals when he was back to school it was Vidhya who initiated a talk with Vivek. He was reluctant in the beginning but soon yielded to her. Five years of friendship, but soon after their school days Vidhya realized that the colour of their bond was not just friendship but something beyond that and it was she who confessed rather proposed him first. The spark in his eyes told her that he too shared the same colour of love with her just as she did.

After completing B Arch and BTech Vidhya and Vivek started exploring their career paths. Soon they got married with both the families' approval. Two years later Eesha was born to them. Life seemed complete, smooth and happy. Vivek even took one year off from his job just to take care of Eesha till her first birthday. He became a wholesome father. Eesha was his little princess and Vivek, her Super Dad. Just two years before, the couple left their jobs and started their own company, 'Eesha Constructions'!

The smile on her face faded when her thoughts went back to their conversation a day before when he told her that he is going abroad seeking better job opportunities and the company has to be taken care of by Vidhya. She was shocked. The rules of their marriage were all broken; no more discussions, opinions, suggestions, only decisions to be agreed upon.

The clock struck 12. Vidhya came to her senses as she heard the door opening. She followed the silent footsteps moving to Eesha's room. There he was, silently looking at his sleeping daughter. He was about to caress her forehead where he stopped in the midway and whispered "Good night, my little princess." Eesha, as if sensing her father's presence turned to his side and murmured back, "Good night, papa", still in her sleep. He gently closed the door behind.

"Vivek, we need to talk."

"It's already midnight, Vidhya. I'm tired. Will talk in the morning.

"Ok, then. We are leaving you and this house tomorrow morning, me and Eesha."

"What?" Vivek gasped for breath.

"Just cut the drama, Vivek! Don't tell me you are spending late night in the office, working; don't tell me you are going abroad to earn more. The Vivek I know will not prioritize money over relationships, money over family." Anger and pain mingled in her voice.

"Vidhya, please understand..." Words left him abruptly.

Vidhya came near him, hugged him tight, "Only I can understand you better than anyone else in this world. No secrets between us so far. Don't break our rules. There is something tormenting you in and out. It's killing us. It's destroying our child. Even she started noticing your neglect. It's my mistake. I should have asked you about this in the first place, months back. I'm sorry, I left you alone in pain. Let's share it now. Believe me, I will be there with you whatever it is. Let's sort this out together. Finally, we need you back..."

His tears made her shoulder wet and she realized he is getting ready. He hugged her tight. She pressed him gently and waited.

An hour later, sipping their usual stress buster, the cold coffee Vidhya had made, accompanied by the cool breeze from the balcony with his love leaning towards him on his shoulder, Vivek opened up the secret pain that he was carrying all through out these months.

"Vidhya, you remember the night we celebrated our Eesha's last birthday?"

"How can I forget that night which turned our life upside down?" The darkness in the air slowly covered Vidhya's eyes.

Eesha was lying between them, tired after the party. It was almost 2 o' clock in the morning that they suddenly woke up seeing her shivering. It was high fever. They immediately rushed her to the hospital. The next two days whatever was done, the fever didn't subside. Later it was found to be pneumonia. Even the doctors were a bit apprehensive and doubtful about her situation. The hopeless days, the sleepless nights they spent only with the strength of prayers. They got their life back finally when Eesha was recovered completely a month after.

"The day which took a worst turn in my life as a father." Vivek's crushed voice brought Vidhya back to the present.

"The day which reminded me of an incident narrated by my grandmother, years back. I always longed for my father's love throughout my life. That craving was more during my childhood. Just like any other boy of my age, I always wanted my father to play with me, crack jokes with me and take me out and have fun. But all were just dreams which never came true. The existence of our relationship was felt only through a nod of agreement, a smile which was always imprisoned on his lips but never escaped or a faint glimmer in his eyes on my achievements. It's not like I had to endure a loveless life for I had my mother who poured endless love and care for me. But even then, something was missing and maybe I'm destined to live with that emptiness throughout.

I revealed my doubt once, to my grandmother. Why my father is not expressive of his love to me?

Is it because he is a military man? Army men can be tough and strict but that don't mean them to refrain from loving their dear ones."

"That may not be the only reason, my dear", I heard my grandmother say with a faint smile on her lips.

"Only love reciprocates love. How can we give something to someone when we are loaded barren of the same?", She went on. Your father was deprived of his father's love in his childhood. Not only him, his four other siblings too. No, if I say their father had not loved them, it would be the greatest sin!" She sighed. "The fact was that he exhibited himself to be impassive. He loved his children more than anything else in this world. His world revolved around his family. But he was afraid to love."

"Afraid to love?"

"Yes, afraid to love, afraid to lose ..." With an agonizing pain she recounted.

Vivek's grandparents were blessed with six children; three daughters and three sons including his father among which only one was fortunate enough to get her father's love as immensely as it was and that was his great aunt, their eldest daughter, their first born; Janaki, their own Jani. She added meaning to their life; their only means of love and joy. She was even given the freedom to call her parents by their names; Devi and Krishnan.

It was her sixth birthday, that day. Jani appeared to be an angel in her pink frock with her hair braided on both sides adorned with jasmine flowers.

"Amma, I want to sleep in the cradle listening to your song. Will you do that for me?", Jani frolicked after the lunch, after the celebration. Devi was surprised to hear her daughter calling her 'Amma' for the first time in her life. With a smile, she made a cradle with her saree, let her daughter in and started singing her favourite song. "Wake me up when Appa comes", Jani said as sleep started covering her little eyes. Hours passed and Jani didn't wake up. It was her last sleep, in fact, a much longer one. It was later found out that the girl had a weak heart, much softer one, which was unable to bear the strength of her body. Devi wailed profusely, remembering each and every moment she had with her daughter. But Krishnan remained silent, no tears, no words. He didn't even let anyone touch his daughter's body. He carried her in his arms to the back yard, dug the ground himself; kept her inside and covered it with the soil. That day he not only had buried his daughter but also himself as a father, the death of ever smiling, cool headed, light hearted Krishnan.

It took years for him to come back to life again but he was never the same as before. After that incident none had seen him smiling or crying. He was slowly turning to a man with no feelings. Years of stress and trauma made him believe that it was his intense love for his daughter that killed her. She was unable to bear the burden of love, he concluded which made him never show his attachments to his younger sons and daughters afraid that would kill them too.

"What if history repeats? What if my love for my daughter will put her life in danger? May be, I'm superstitious, maybe I'm not thinking normal but I don't want to risk my daughter's life for anything in this world. That day from the hospital I decided to stay away from her, from you, just for her safety. I'm such an unfortunate father". Vivek's voice quivered as he cried loudly.

Unable to say a word, Vidhya looked at him with utmost love, empathy and concern. She rubbed his shoulders, stood with him silent, letting him pour his heart out the strain and pain that he had accumulated inside him all these days.

****

"You cannot catch me, Papa, try if you can", Eesha was running fast as she could on the beach with Vivek after her.

Sitting on the sands, seeing them playing with the waves, Vidhya's heart too rose high with the spirits once lost.

It's almost a month after that incident. Now Vivek is under Dr Chris' treatment, a renowned Psychiatrist in the city. It was hard for Vivek to believe in the beginning that what he was undergoing was trauma that too transmitted from generation to generation; from his grandfather to his father and later from his father to him. Slowly he started accepting the fact as there is no other way other than to accept the reality, the final truth. The so-called life itself is a mystery; it's not only the chords of love but the chain of hatred, doubt, fear, anxiety can also bind people from generation to generation, which can even ruin their lives eventually.

On and on, Vivek started reflecting on the doctor's words as it is up to him and in his hands whether to pass that baggage of trauma to the next generation or to discard it wholly, only for a better survival. Thus, finally he decided to end his role as a victim by coming out of that generational curse. It will take time to heal the once inflicted pain. In that stress of withdrawal and the strain of pulling out, one will learn about selfcare, self-love, for there are times in life only we can help ourselves out while all others can merely stand as viewers. It's in our hands to rise from just being a victim to the victor; the only way to change the destiny. There is hope as long as there is a will to confront the pain and a heart with warmth to love again and again, no matter what.

"Papa, you know what, you are the best dad ever in this world." Eesha voiced out kissing her father's cheeks.

"And you are my little princess forever..." Vivek hugged her with his one arm with all the love he had. With his other arm around Vidhya, he winked at her, "Thank you and love you forever".

******

PS: The characters in the story are fully fictional but the situation mentioned above has its close resemblance to a real-life incident. Intergenerational Trauma is an inherited trauma that is the result of a traumatic event or situation which may affect multiple generations. It can lead to anxiety, loss of interest, isolation and even depression. Definitely, a person who goes through this trauma can break the cycle and heal from it with the support of an expert and strong will. Feel free to open up your fear and get help so that you knowingly or unknowingly don't pass this trauma to the next generation.

Author- Lakshmy

Lakshmy : An Educator, Author, an Orator and a bookaholic whose intense love for thoughts words and creative art has facilitated her to carve articles, poems and short stories on varied themes.

She also serves as a member of WICCI, Co-founder of WeTalk Child Rights and Editor and Manuscript Specialist of WeTalk Literary Agency.

Being the author of Reveries Unbound, a book of Poems on seeking self and Co Author of five anthologies previously published by We Talk, she has unveiled her virtuosity in moulding diverse characters, giving life to multifarious plots. A wanderlust but most of her journeys are inward, into the complex core of human mind which makes her stories reflective, meditative and her dramatic personae always loaded with multi dimensional emotions.

CHAPTER FOUR

The First Born

The early morning sunbeams filtered through the mango tree and laid a sequined tapestry on the emerald water. Little Bonhi's heart jumped and skipped a beat or two, to see the floating array of spangles bobbing up and down, like a fluid mosaic, as Moral and Morali, the swan couple, slid into the pond. They were a pair so beautiful and elegant; the curvature of their slender necks was akin to a sculptor's masterpiece, and their glistening white streamlined bodies were symbolic of boundless beauty and aesthetic appeal. Bonhi would watch them in adoration and admiration. The cob-pen duo had their cygnets following in a single-file line of fluff balls. Disciplined yet endearing, each youngling mimicked the parents' movements. The charm of the procession doubled with their reflections on the water. Bonhi was in awe of the swan family.

"Bonhi, come over and help me with the vegetables" called out her mother, Manashi, in a stern voice. Bonhi quickly ran across the courtyard into the kitchen. She pulled out the big "*boti*"[1], and with all the expertise a seven-year-old kid could have, she started cutting the vegetables her mother wanted to cook for that day. That was her daily, morning regime. Her young restless mind wandered off with Morali and her babies on a glittery water ride.

"Aaahhh!", cried Bonhi. Manashi instantly snapped "Again your mind is abstracted? you are so careless and unmindful! Go and get some ointment on your cut. Always daydreaming!" As Bonhi walked out she heard her mother saying "Ufff, this girl is good for nothing!". Little Bonhi's sensitive heart sank, the remark was more hurtful than the cut on her finger.

The swans' unconditional and unwavering love for their cygnets was a testament to Bonhi that parents' love knew no boundaries. Morali laid her eggs in a bush, with an overlay of rush and reeds, by the pond. Moral would bring food for her and take turns incubating the eggs patiently for days together, till the hatchlings came out. The bond they shared was so enduring and close-knit. Morali would cover her babies with her soft downy feathers and feed each of them in turn during the nesting period. Both parents played active roles in caring for and nurturing their young ones. They taught them how to waddle, paddle and swim. Bonhi saw the cycle several times and knew it thoroughly.

Manashi, a teacher, at a school in the small town of Bashirhat, was strict and disciplined, even more so as a mother. She was aiming for the position of headmistress, after all, her years of hard work should not go wasted. Her daughters were 2 years apart in age, Bonhi the elder one and Sharmi the younger. They attended the same school where she taught. Manab, her husband and father of the two sisters was quite indifferent towards family affairs. Manashi had trained her elder daughter to take care of the household chores and to look after her younger sibling, while she was busy, away, or needed a helping hand. Sharmi the younger one was spared of all these responsibilities and tasks. Little Bonhi would do all her duties diligently and lovingly, she never complained, even if she felt tired by the end of the day. She was always over-enthusiastic and felt glad to be of any help around the house.

Moral-Morali were vigilant about their brood and safeguarded them. It was a stunning sight to see them spreading their white pristine wings giving shelter to their babies from rain or gusty wind. Their wingspan was an immaculate blend of grace, purity, love and care which transcended and elevated parenthood to a celestial plane, close to divinity. Bonhi found this profundity awe-inspiring. When the ducklings grew older the parents taught them how to forage for food in the muddy ground and pond water. They would dabble with their rumps sticking out of the water while they fed, Bonhi thought they resembled little kids exploring tide pools. Mirroring the sisters when they go collecting clams from the mud flats of the Ichhamati River.

On holidays the siblings played around in the courtyard, under the mango tree, by the pond. Bonhi had dozed off in the cool breeze under the mango tree one day. When Manashi happened to see Bonhi peacefully sleeping, she pulled her by the arm and slapped her hard across the face. The still groggy little kid took a while to realise what went wrong. Manashi shouted "How can you sleep and not take care of your little sister? you irresponsible brat! If something untoward had happened?!" Bonhi's inner voice promptly asked, "You were also sleeping ma?! If I had drowned? Who would have saved me?". But she just said with tears welling up in her big brown eyes, "Sorry Ma, I will never make this mistake again". Bonhi ran to the backyard and cried under the banyan tree. She had not shown up till late evening. She breathed a sigh of relief when she realized no one had missed her or noticed her long absence, she escaped another round of scolding, she thought. But there was a throbbing pain deep down somewhere inside of her. No one felt her absence!

The cygnets would play with the cormorants who occasionally visited the pond. They would dive and come to the surface splashing water on each other. They resembled a group of ballet dancers in glittery tinseled outfits creating an ethereal visual poetry. The extraordinary yet sublime beauties of nature overwhelmed Bonhi and fulfilment washed over her. She enjoyed their company. The swan couple watched over their kids' mischief and would put a check when required. Their trumpeting calls with different pitches and sounds were a language the younglings understood and reciprocated in obedience with their cute chirps and whistles. Vocalising was such an integral part of their family dynamics, reinforcing bonds, ensuring safety and coordinating. Why was articulating so difficult for Bonhi, she would often ponder. Moral-Morali were an embodiment of nurture and care, love and affection, in Bonhi's perception.

The captivating Autumn season was Bonhi's favourite. The warmth of summer and the humid monsoon transition in grandeur into chilly crispiness in the air. Harvest festivals, Durga Pujo, and Diwali all fall in Autumn. Most importantly she loved the Kaash phool (Kans grass) in full bloom during this time of the year. Along the banks of the Ichhamoti River, in tufts of feathery plumes, they swayed in the slightest breeze, forming silvery waves. Her fluttering heart would sing in rhythm with the dancing inflorescences. Sometimes she would break a kaash-phool strand and run, holding her hand high in the air. The tiny silky white bristles would fly over her head as if a bunch of butterflies. She would run along the riverbank, the lace of her skirt following her like the remnants of her dream.

Breathless at the doorstep she exclaimed in excitement at her discovery "Look ma look! Baba[2] see how the flowers are turning into butterflies!"

The wise parents laughed, and Manashi blurted in disgust at her crazy imagination "*Dosh bochhor hoye gelo, Ei meye tar ar buddhi shuddhi hobena*" (Completed ten years, but this girl will always remain an empty head)!

"Go and get some lessons in your head instead", Manab said tautly "What would your sister learn from you? To be a loser?"

Bonhi quietly went back to her room that day, trying to wrap her head around, how it was her onus to be an ideal for her younger sibling. Why was it not enough to love and care for her!? Why was it important to stand out from others?! Why could she not be just herself?! She turned around after every couple of steps, hoping to see Baba or Ma coming behind her to help her with her studies, ask her questions about Palashir Judhyo (Battle of Plassey), all the mountain ranges of India, how infections are caused in birds and animals, how mother birds incubated their eggs and took care of the hatchlings till they grew up. Why kaash phool is not a flower but a bunch of tiny flowers. Bonhi knew it all! She knew all her lessons and more. And she wanted to show it to her parents. She longed for her parents to understand her and acknowledge her worth. She wished to tell her parents she would be a singer one day. But she could not vocalise, she could not articulate her feelings, and her voice would always locked inside of her and drown into oblivion eventually. She craved for them to be like the swan parents impartial, non-judgmental, loving and nurturing.

The demeaning treatment, belittling her for everything was supposedly the usual norm of the house. These were usually not done deliberately by the parents, but in their ignorance, they were causing immense damage to a child's mind. Bonhi would hang her head in shame, a bruised rain lily, so that no one could get a glimpse of her teary eyes. She wanted to dump all her embarrassment and cover them up with a pile of dry Autumn leaves. She wished that the wind would carry the leaves, laden with hurt and rebuke to a faraway land, and rot. But the more she tried to hide and suppress, the more weeds of pain and rejection grew within her. In the process, her self-confidence, and self-esteem were savagely trampled and crushed. She felt mentally burnt out. Her existence was a dying echo in an abandoned bottomless well.

After three years Bonhi entered the transitional phase of her life, like one season slipping and sliding into the next. From tweenhood to teenagehood. In this phase, kids show an array of emotions. It is much the same as a roller coaster ride for them. Their fragile minds and thoughts are like the Dandelion clock hanging delicately on a central stem. A little blow, a careless shove can have them all break and scatter in the mayhem. They are like splinters which are ready to set ablaze. They walk the precarious precipice, with one side the lush green rolling meadows and on the other a steep treacherous cliff. A little imbalance or lack of emotional support, care and supervision could end up in devastating consequences of their mindset and behaviourism.

The rude comparisons, the taunting opinionated statements about how she was not an ideal role model to her younger sister, how she needed to sacrifice and compromise being the elder one, that she should set good examples, all these suffocated her, stifled her sensitive being. She would want to protest, but her voice would get muffled and strangled in thick, rough yarns of judgmental overviews.

Manab returned home early one day and found Bonhi murmuring incoherently *"Baba, porabe? Khawabe Ma?! Morali aaye! Kaashphool! Projapoti..."*[3] Then she drifted into delirium. As he went closer and found she was burning with fever, he wasted no time and scooped her in his arms and took her to the doctor. The doctor was unable to find an underlying infection or cause for her high temperature. Several diagnostic tests were done. Everything seemed normal for a prognosis. Bonhi had to be hospitalized. She recovered from that spell of fever, but something was not the same anymore. Nothing about her was the same anymore.

She was a butterfly going into reverse metamorphosis-against nature's norms. The sprightly, bubbly kid had woven a chrysalis of resentment around her. She was withdrawing herself into a hard shell. The feeling of emotional abandonment is an invisible wound, caused by repeated stabs of disconnect and deprivation from her family. Humiliation had drained her self-love. She felt unloved, dejected and shattered by those whom she loved the most. She would often skip school with the excuse of stomach pain and diarrhoea. Her withdrawal and internalizing were manifested into frequent bouts of high fever. The parents were oblivious to Bonhi's symptoms of "abandonment disorder", they ignored them as teenage tantrums, dramatics and mood swings.

Bonhi's cocooned temperament was like the lull before a storm. The unsettling phase where her mind was suspended in a fragile equilibrium. That calm soon got converted into an inverted rage. Filled with self-doubt, she started blaming herself for being unworthy of love, and she tried inflicting pain on herself. Bonhi's inner voice would outcry in hatred and anger "Give me back my childhood, give me back my dreams!" And then she would become violent and aggressive, as if she despised everyone around her, even herself. Destroying things, breaking whatever was within her reach. Her indignation and outrage exceeded and went beyond control.

Bonhi was taken to a rehabilitation centre for mental treatment and care. The damage to her mind was so deeply seeded that she had to be given electroconvulsive therapy (ECT or electric shock treatment) to calm her down. Manashi resigned from the position of Headmistress and quit her job. Manab's repentance never came to an end "*Amaye khoma korte parbi na*"[4] he would say now and then as if talking to himself.

Bonhi might have forgiven her parents, but will Manab and Manashi be able to forgive themselves?! Bonhi suffered from short-term memory loss, the side effects of ECT! Or was it her deliberate attempt to forget every bit of her past?!

Bonhi's dream of becoming a singer was trapped in the loop of her endless murmur. Her heart probably still cries for love and longs for a healing embrace, we don't know, because she doesn't allow anyone to come close to her. At the sight of her parents, she gets convulsions and seizures. Prolonged emotional abandonment scarred her mind in a way that resembled an insane pattern of ink blotches on a blotting paper. Bonhi is far from her reality and her dreams, what one could see now are the reflections of her fragmented soul.

****

Glossary

1. *Boti: a plank of wood with a big foldable sharp knife attached to one end, used for cutting vegetables and fruits, usually in a Bengali household.*
2. *Baba: father in Bengali.*
3. *Baba, porabe? Khawabe Ma?!Morali aaye! Kaashphool! Projapoti..!: Baba, will you teach me? Feed me Ma?! Morali come! Kaashphool! Butterflies...!*
4. *Amaye khoma korte parbi na?: will you not be able to forgive me?!*

Author- Saswati Sinha

Saswati Sinha is a mother, educationist, entrepreneur, a child psychologist and holds a PhD in medical microbiology. She has a quirky sense of storytelling which has made her a favourite amongst kids over the last one and half decades. She loves writing anecdotes, diaries, and comic strips. She has authored several scientific articles and research papers. In this anthology, her stories highlight mental health conditions we undergo but often ignore the gravitas of the same. Intending to sensitize one and all to the importance of mental well-being she hopes that her readers will have valuable takeaways from this anthology.

CHAPTER FIVE

Anastasis: An Awakening Within

"Hey Garima, I have no clue who you are, and I have no idea why FB repeatedly keeps sending suggestions about you. But upon visiting your profile, I could sense strong positive vibrations! You have a very strong aura, and more importantly, you have given me a timely well-needed positivity boost, when I needed it the most. Thanks, my friend!"

As usual, whenever bored, Garima used to check the spam folder of her messenger, and today she found this message. She used to get many messages from strangers, but this one she was reading, she felt was different from the rest. It was a long one and she felt some genuinity in it. She stared at it for some time and smiled.

Generally, she never replies to any spam messages. Reading them was her hobby these days. At times, she would read them and just ignore them. She particularly liked to read the long messages few people send. Some used to tell her how beautiful she was, few wanted to know if she was single and ready to mingle, and there were also a few men who would send her vulgar pictures and messages. She despised such messages, she would block them and delete those messages. Still, she went through the spam messages from time to time to feel good about herself! She wanted to reconfirm those men still yearned for her and desired her. This became her escape mechanism for her from her mundane life. However, today she felt she should be sending a reply to this particular one. She visited the sender's profile, and though the profile was locked it had something special and she felt an immediate connection. Even though she had the urge to start a conversation, she restricted herself and just replied with a thanks. She logged out of her Facebook profile which is dormant these days. Once upon a time, she was very social and active on all the social media platforms. She used to write about social issues, and stories, and even used to post her pictures online. But those who knew her suddenly noticed the change in her after her marriage.

Garima was known for her infectious smile and warm nature. She always had been a perfectionist, who excelled in her studies, pursued a demanding career, and maintained a social life. She was a classical dancer, writer and activist. Sometimes her own expectations grew heavier for her. In her growing-up phase, anxiety was her constant companion and depression lurked her in the shadows. But every time she rose from the ashes like a phoenix stronger.

Her marriage with Anand was an arranged one, the best alliance her parents could find for her. His job, family status everything matched with their status. Garima was not excited though, after a trail of broken relationships and heartbreaks she decided she would at least let the parents be happy, so she agreed to whichever proposal they brought. Anand was not particularly her type of person. He had an average look and was very soft-spoken, and ambitious. Garima on the other hand, had a striking beauty, captivating eyes, and a charismatic charm that drew people to her like moths to the flame. She was the centre of attention wherever she went. The wedding was the talk of the town, Garima's dad threw the best reception and the groom was gifted with a brand-new sedan and a new flat in Bangalore, where they both were going to start their family. Garima did not oppose anything. She was too numb to all that was happening around her. The activist inside her took a dormant state. On her normal self, she would have revolted against her dad for gifting the groom. She was dead against dowry and such systems. But in this case, Garima knew that the groom and family never asked for anything but it was her dad's inflated pride which wanted to show off. All these years he was waiting for this. Garima decided to give her best for this new start. She became the best wife to Anand, trying to understand his likes and dislikes. More than her job she invested time in setting up her new family life. They were seemingly a happy couple.

After a few months of the marriage, Garima sensed an unmistakable resemblance between Anand and her father. Anand was undoubtedly a loving husband most of the time, but she saw a different personality at times. She realised he wanted to be the centre of attraction all the time, everything starts and ends with him. He had an obsession with himself. She saw him spending hours admiring himself in front of the mirror. He considered himself as the most magnificent man walking on this earth. If she failed to make his favourite dish or failed to make him happy, she saw a completely different person in him. She kept her patience and thought things would fall into place. All these years she used to write on her blogs, Facebook and other online platforms and raised her voice against what she felt was not right. She was so shocked that she was not able to do that now. Anand had asked her to keep away from all the social media platforms. He said she was getting unnecessary male attention, and hence she did not log in to her social media accounts after that. Meanwhile, she became pregnant and she thought once the baby arrived, she would have a better life.

Tara came into their life as a fresh breath of air. Everything was going smoothly now. Anand was such an adoring father, from changing the diaper to getting up and helping her to feed the baby, he took care of everything, Garima too by now quit her job so that she could give quality time to her baby. Five years went by smoothly, now Tara was going to the nursery. Once again, Garima felt the narcissist personality in Anand was peeping out. Like earlier, he was spending hours together in front of the mirror. He started finding flaws with Garima. Over time, Garima understood that he was very clever and well-calculated. In front of others, he was such an adoring and loving husband that everyone would say she was so lucky to have him. He always manipulated and played games with her and always got away with whatever he wanted. He never forgets to surprise her with expensive gifts such as LV or Gucci bags, expensive perfumes and other branded stuff. She was feeling suffocated. She never wanted any of those. She just wanted to be loved and given respect.

Whenever she tried to confront him, he would say that she misunderstood him. He blame gamed her, and sometimes she doubted herself playing the victim. He tells her that she is so sensitive, and she is imagining things. At times he spends weeks flattering her and building her confidence, only to crash it down with double the effect. Every time she promised herself that this would never happen again, but she would fall for his luring words again because she genuinely loved him.

Two days passed by since she had received the message from the stranger, and she had replied to him saying, "Thanks for the compliment and I'm happy that I could bring some positivity to someone unknown." From that day she had read that message a hundred times in her mind and the stranger's image came to her every now and then. She tried to distract herself from thinking about it but in vain. Finally, she decided to check if any new messages came from him. She liked his name as well, Siddhartha. Her favourite book has been Herman Hesse's 'Siddhartha.' At times she had identified herself with the character Kamala. She logged in to FB Messenger and checked for new messages, her heart skipped a beat when she saw Siddhartha highlighted in the chats, she knew he had sent some message. She clicked on the message and read it aloud. His messages were filled with positivity and she felt elated for the moment. They started exchanging messages. Now it became a daily routine for her, every day she waited for the messages from Siddhartha, it gave her a new ray of hope, and what she lacked in life was revived through these conversations. She felt being heard and being listened to, she started sharing everything with him, and he too gave his ears to her. Also, he was good at analysing the situations and he gave her many suggestions too.

Siddhartha made her realise that from childhood she was in trauma-bonding relationships. Upon discussing her life with Siddhartha, Garima realised that her dad and Anand had unmistakably similar traits. She realised both of them were pernicious. They were hostile, destructive, vindictive and malicious! She glided down memory lane and remembered how her father was never happy with her and her achievements. He always controlled her and criticised her. She excelled in dance and music but her hobbies were non-existent to him. She also remembered how her dad used to treat her mother. He demeaned her in every possible way. Her mother was always torn between his love and his torture. She could never choose between staying or leaving. She always felt ignored, uncared and unimportant. And Garima could see that her marital life was no different. Anand was suffocating her daily. She had become dependent on him so much that she had forgotten her existence. To this day she used to think she was delusional and that she needed a therapist. But chatting with Siddhartha solved many of her problems. For the first time, she realised that all these years she needed to be heard. The conversations with Siddhartha made her feel confident about herself. He told her to pursue her hobbies, and upon his insistence, she started practising dance and started writing. Earlier writing gave her the power to express herself. Suddenly once again she felt empowered and a ray of hope flickered in her sky. Garima's laughter became more genuine and her smile radiated true happiness these days.

Siddhartha also advised her to make a comparative study between her father and Anand. She kept a notebook and started drawing their comparisons and differences. She realised, at first even though she felt they were very similar, they were way apart from each other. Anand though had narcissistic traits, yet he was much more compassionate towards others, especially towards Tara. He would leave no stone unturned when it came to her. He was indeed an adoring father. His behaviour towards her too was not as toxic as her dad's. She had witnessed her dad being physically abusive to her mother. When she mentioned these traits of theirs, to Siddhartha, he assured her that

Anand could be changed through love and counselling. He told her to give Anand a chance and check for the changes in him. She too loved Anand so much and genuinely wanted him to realise that he was going through a mental health issue and wanted him to come out of it.

Garima knew that this was a journey that they both had to cover together and she wanted to give him company throughout. Now her biggest challenge was to let Anand know that he needed help from a therapist. Since Garima was a good storyteller and used to put her words into amazing stories, and Anand was her first reader and critic always. She thought she would use her writing as a tool. She carefully crafted a story which depicted his character and flaws and without blaming she brought up the issue, and the solution as well. She very carefully used each word, and finally gave it to Anand to read and give his opinion. She waited eagerly for him to read and share his opinion. However, even after four days, he did not say a word. Usually, he reads it immediately and gives his suggestions. This time Garima was super anxious, but she did not get any response from Anand. However, today Garima thought she would ask him. When he was back from work, she made his favourite snacks for the evening tea. They sat down for tea together, but before Garima could open the conversation, Anand spoke. He told her that he read the story over and over again and a few things struck him. Garima was all listening with her heart pounding faster. He looked very serious and genuine, and at that moment Garima understood that she had hit the bull's eye. The whole evening Anand sat with her and he discussed that he feels that Garima's character is a reflection of him and that he realised he has this issue. Also, he pleaded to her that he needed help. Over the conversation, Anand explained to her how from childhood at various points in his life he dealt with an inferiority complex and to overcome it he took refuge as a narcissist. He told her that her story made him think and he feels that he is going through a mental ailment and he genuinely feels he needed some help. He assured her he wanted to lead a normal life with her and Tara. He also told her how much he loved them both, and he would take any measures to live a happy life with them. He poured his heart in front of her and he asked if she would give him support. She was waiting for this moment. She hugged him and promised him that she would be walking beside him throughout his journey. She told him that in some way or the other, we all are mentally challenged and only a few of us realise that the problem is real and get the help. She assured him the earlier we acknowledged it and sought help, the easier it was.

The next few days they both researched thoroughly and found out the best psychiatrist in the town and visited her. Garima was so busy for the next few months, that she and Anand took the step together, and she stood by him as a strong pillar. Within a few months, she saw a drastic change in Anand. They were taking a new path in their life. She had almost forgotten about her FB friend Siddhartha. Suddenly she realised it had been months since she chatted with him. She wanted to tell him all the progress in her life. She knew he would be so happy for her. Also, she felt a little guilty that she did not inform him of any of these earlier. She felt she was being so selfish. When she wanted to be heard, was she using him as an audience for her agonies? But when the most important step she took in her life that too upon his advice how she easily had forgotten him! She cursed herself for being so selfish. She opened her messenger eagerly to see his messages, but to her surprise or dismay, she could not find his name in the chats. Instead, she saw the name as 'Facebook User' and she could see only her replies. No messages from the other end were available any more. She was taken aback! Did she really chat to someone all these days or all of this was just her imagination?

Author- Hema Nair

Hema Nair is a writer, blogger, life-skills trainer, philanthropist and a vivid traveller, based out of Manila, Philippines. She has done her Masters in English Literature and Language and PGD in Journalism. She has worked as a corporate trainer at Infosys BPO, Bangalore. Her interests are writing, learning, unlearning, and re-learning, travelling, studying human behaviour/nature, exploring ancient history, reading, and dreaming. She describes herself as a dreamer by day and a thinker by night. She is married to Idhayan and is a mother to a 14-year-old lovely daughter Dia.

CHAPTER SIX

One More Round!!

Part 1: The Coach's View

"Box" – the word shouted by the referee bought Jay out of the trance that he had gone in.

Of late, Jay had fallen into the habit of going out to the sports complex, sitting by the ringside for hours together, absently looking at the ring, the boxers sparring in it, he would occasionally glance at the folks outside the ring, some shadowing, some hitting the mitts whilst some going after the bag to give the much-required final touches and the conditioning to their preparation. While the newbies jumped ropes and some struggled with their footwork.

Unknown to him, whilst he would look at the familiar surroundings, the usual cacophony of people around him, the other trainers, and senior players would, amongst themselves, joke about him, some cracked jokes openly, some in a more hushed manner. All save one, the seniormost coach at the Athletic Sports Complex, Jay's coach, mentor, and godfather when it came to ring knowledge – Coach Almeida looked at Jay with a look that was a caricature of half of concern and the remainder of anger. Concern as to what was wrong with his protégé' given the time he had been away from the ring and anger some at Jay and most at himself as to how Jay was wasting his talent and how Coach was not able to do anything about it as he was not one of those who'd let talent slip by, let alone get wasted, especially in his presence and him being helpless to make a difference.

Coach Benjamin Almeida had trained Jay (and had grown fond of him) since an early age. He remembered very clearly the day he had stepped into the Meadows school a few years ago as a part of an initiative to promote sports in school children's lives and Boxing as a way of life. He recalled that he had stepped into class 8C, which, as per the principal, had the most mischievous children. As usual, he walked in, in his tracksuit, opened up with the students about sports that they loved, and then to his dismay, when he began speaking on the topic of contact sports and how Boxing as a sport would be beneficial for them, both as a sport and a way of life, the enthusiasm turned to nonchalant participation, the general perception of Boxing after all was that of a sport for those who had a penchant for blood and violence and such people usually had cracked noses, broken jaws and missing teeth.

So, as he was about to move out, slightly dejected, he saw one hand raised among the strength of 28 students, turning around he saw, he saw a young Jay, who posed him a question – "My parents say that there is no career in sports in India, is there a career in Boxing?". The wily coach found himself saying– Come to the Gym and find out for yourself if you are worth enough to make a career in sports... in Boxing.

And sure enough, the coach's word stuck in the young boy's mind, and he found himself in the ASC's indoor stadium in front of boxing rings. The coach clearly remembered the expression on the child's face, it was the look of someone who had finally found where they belonged and not one of trepidation or awe.

Coach Almeida snapped out of the past and wondered to himself, will this guy ever be able to come back and do justice to his potential? After all, it was his dream to make it to the medal podium of the nationals for which he had been prepping... putting in all his blood, sweat, and tears since day one, and now it had been more than 2 years that he had even done any roadwork, forget rest of the practice. His growing paunch clearly showed it.

Part 2 – The Rise & Fall

Jay Bisht, 23 years old, despite being 6'1" was stockily built, unlike typical boxers who rely on speed, Jay had also conditioned himself for power by frequently training with weights, an approach that the others in his team abhorred as they considered that a boxer who would train with weights was bound to "Muscle" his punches and would in all likelihood injure himself in that process, hence, as a tradition, they relied on speed and agility.

Growing up in a middle-class family, Jay was no different than any other kid on the block, weak at Math but strong in the rest of the subjects, Jay had a natural affinity for Biology and sports. Like any other kid of his age in a cricket-crazy nation, he too loved cricket and was a natural when it came to the game. Jay believed strongly in meritocracy and it was a harsh eye-opener for him when, on the happiest day of his life, upon being selected to be a part of the playing 11 for a state-level tournament (one that had the potential to take him to places), he was asked for a sponsor details, failing which he would have to self-sponsor, that meant that the family would have to come up with half a million (somewhere around 5 Lakhs). An amount that was out of the realm of affordability for any middle-class family, especially a sport. Indian parents usually being disinclined to the idea of their children going after sports instead of focusing hard on studies, Jay knew that his parents were no exception, so with a half-hearted approach, he had breached the idea to his family and the reaction was as expected.

His mother was shell-shocked and broke down, his father as usual, in a gruff and non-plussed manner shrugged and told him "If you can come up with the amount by yourself, go ahead, consider us with you. But don't expect I would shell out that amount for you, especially for whim for cricket. Instead, focus and make something better out of yourself."

This was nothing new to young Jay, except for another attempt. But his spirit was broken and his heart was no longer in cricket when he couldn't make it in the playing 11 owing to lack of sponsorship and unable to pay the required amount. Not one to give up, he resolved that he would get into a sport where he can make a difference by himself, instead of relying on others to make it.

When Coach Almeida came into his class shortly after this incident, Jay's thoughts changed into resolve as he listened to what the coach was saying and to the dismay of his classmates (one trying to pull his hand down) he had found himself raising his hand and asking the coach the question that changed his life and took him to avenues that not only gave him exposure as a sportsman but also taught him about life and mindset. However, on the other hand, his relationship with his family deteriorated, being averse to the idea of sports as a career, his family was completely aghast at their only son getting into a contact sport with potential negative and long-lasting ramifications – both physical and psychological. Jay attributed this concern to their lack of understanding of the sport. "If you know what you are doing, you reduce the risk by 90%". Was what he told to his family, whenever the need to sidestep arguments and convince them arose.

Coach Almeida, having seen the potential in Jay took Jay under his wings, The young boy soon found out the difference between cricket and boxing. Where one involved sportsmanship with slight sledging to gain an upper hand, the other sport very bluntly taught him that to get an upper edge on his opponent, he had to out-train, out-speed and out-think his opponent, and if not careful, a loss was just one punch away – A philosophy that Jay found similar to when it came to life too.

As days passed on, Jay on one hand, made serious progress as a boxer however, on the other hand, his grades dipped, spending more time in the sport, he began to make a habit of relying on last minute studies to "just" make it through the exams, something that further strained the relationship with his family and dear ones. They say that what you don't get in a family, you find in the world, Jay became best friends with Arvind, a fellow team member and a Welter weight on the rise. They both excelled in their respective weight categories – Jay as a light heavy (75-81 kg) and Arvind as a Welter weight (64-69 kg). Both had begun from school days, were naturals, made state gold in school as well as junior college whilst making their presence felt in the open category representing their state in the nationals too. Soon Jay set his sight on what he would do – make it to the nationals whilst clearing HSC examinations and secure a place in the Indian Army through the sports quota. The calculation was simple, the sports quota recruitment notification was out, selection comprised of 5 stages - shortlisting was basis sports achievements something that jay already had in his kitty by then, next came Physical Efficiency Test, followed Physical Standards Test, the Sports Trials, document verification, and a medical examination. Of the 5 stages, the only difficult part for Jay (and indeed difficult it was) was the trials as those comprised of boxers from all over, the rest as per his thoughts, was a respectable formality.

They say, when you are going strong, you should ensure that you work on the blind spots too whilst you bask in glory. Life struck a knockout blow to Jay, not just one... but multiple and each one was more severe than the other. So severe that he didn't know what hit him, how and why.

Keeping the selections in mind, Jay began his preparation, meticulously and in a totally disciplined manner – his training regimen was divided in to 2 parts – Endurance training and roadwork in the morning and technique practice in the evening. Recovery – a good night's sleep (which was a rarity for him considering the errands that he would run in order to compensate for his contribution in his house).

As the competition dates drew to a close, his regimen became even more rigorous, Roadwork became 8 kilometers run every morning with weekends dedicated to a 15-kilometer pure endurance. The evening training that initially comprised of shadow boxing and footwork now progress on to mitts, bag and finally - sparring. All this was done keeping his weight in line with the light heavy weight category as he knew, a mere 100 grams above or below the prescribed limits meant disqualification (as you cannot have more than one person in a weight category).

Come selection day, Jay at the outset and as anticipated, had known that in this outing his weight category had a formidable line up, but that was what he was waiting for and preparing for wasn't he.

Downtime waiting for your weight category matches to begin was the worst, everyone knew it and everyone disliked it. 3rd day into the competitions was when the list for the light heavyweight category was put on display. The first two didn't interest Jay, the 3rd one did – it was Jay's against Dilip Yadav. Looking further down, he knew the route, a total of 4 bouts before he hit the medal rounds, a quick calculation of 3 minutes with 1 minute break of 3 rounds multiplied by 4 matches got the tally to 48 minutes of pure, unbridled action to reach his goal of getting selected.

30 minutes before his scheduled bout, Jay took a corner with his coach and Arvind for warm up and final prep – he knew his corner, so the red kit along with the red coloured boxing shoes was already donned. he removed the track suit, got his inner wraps (or the crepes as they are lovingly called) on, on his hands so that the required structural support to his wrists, hands and forearms was in place, next came the gloves, the headgear and last was the gum shield that he would put on, once he was in the ring just before the bout began.

Jay got in the ring for his first bout, the gum shield went in, he went ahead, the referee called out the rules, checked both boxers to confirm whether they had worn their gum shields and protective cups. The handshake happened and both were sent back to their respective corners. The lights dimmed, the bell rang and both fighters came charging at each other. Jay always preferred to meet his opponent in the centre and avoid corners at all costs, for a corner was one way to get caught up in an onslaught and get bust up, and before you know it, you are done for. He used the same approach here as well, took a few jabs, felt and weighed the "fight" in his opponent, it was 30 seconds to go for the 1st

round that jay identified an opening and got a strategy in place. The bell rang, signalling the end of the first round.

In the one-minute break, Arvind came in to the ring, removed the gum shield and quickly discussed the next round strategy with Jay, it was agreed by them both that the moment his opponent dips his right hand for an upper cut, Jay would go after him with a left hook, KO and the bout is won. Both agreed, but the coach's eye had identified something else and he told Jay from the ringside to wait it out till the final round.

Jay in his fervour went for kill soon as the bell rang, he saw his opponent dip his hand for the uppercut and went for the hook, only to be decoyed and step right in a full-blown left hook of his opponent, world went black as Jay went down.

When he came back to consciousness, he found himself out of the ring, Arvind holding smelling salts and an angry coach looking over him (with a hint of concern). While the rest of the team was sympathetic toward his first bout loss, all his coach said was – "That's what happens when you get cocky" Kismat muh pe tamacha maarti hai. And little did both of them knew that that was the only discussion to happen for quite a long time to come.

The loss was not new, but the shame was apparent coupled with a shattered dream, Jay came back to his home town to a family who though were disappointed at their son's loss, secretly rejoiced with a hope that at least now, their son's ways would divert toward studies and a more "stable" career. His father time and again would try to coax him saying "I told you so, Boxing mein kya rakha hai? Tere paas time hai, padh ke 12th clear karle, maybe you might just be able to get in to some decent course like B.Sc.

And Jay knowing that a critical opportunity was out of the window focused on his academics, exams came and went, and then came the day for the results – Jay flunked in 2 subjects – Maths and Physics, the second blow came and came hard.

When the family and friends got wind of this debacle, Jay got the final ultimatum – Give up the thought of boxing and divert all efforts to study if you want to stay here, else go out and live on your own, we can't simply afford to have you in the house. And that's where the third hammer struck.

This trifecta of events took their own toll on Jay and in a fit of anger and frustration he gave up on boxing and redirected all his efforts to clearing his HSC and getting admission to a degree course. He locked up his beloved kit with a resolve that he would never open it and went about his life, totally disconnected from the world of boxing and his fellow ring brothers.

The first few months were a struggle, Jay had a hard time not only catching up with life but also on other fronts, the road to reformation is not easy, there were days that were intolerable when anyone who's anyone passed sarcastic comments on his failing the HSC, his own parents' behaviour confused him. Left him shocked and numbed both by their comments and his reflection on his losses. The initial days, Jay would remain asleep for long hours, and distanced himself from any situations that would involve social contact and a reminder by anyone about these series of events. For a long time, he felt helpless and broken, he would give in to crying. But as the days passed by, the ring and the sports complex got left behind and were replaced with books. Jay was able to clear his HSC, get into a degree course and out of sheer determination, managed to secure a rank in the first year as well. Though it was a phase that depicted an overall change of the personality of a person, deep down Jay knew that something was still amiss and till that was not found out, he could never be able to fully get himself back. He would still keep himself away from societal contact, still felt aimless and at a loss. Just when he felt that he was about to sink in an abyss, he heard a knock on the door of his room that snapped him out of his thoughts, reluctantly, he opened the door to find the same look of dismay on his father's face that had been missing from some time. And as his father took a step aside, he saw Arvind – after more than 2 years.

Soon as Jay's parents reluctantly left, Kaisa hai Champ? Arvind said with the same old tone and the same old meaning. Tera toh pet nikal aaya hai be, chuckled Arvind whilst he hugged Jay who though reciprocated the gesture, reminded himself not to take the bait.

Exchanging pleasantries and reminiscing old times, Arvind then revealed his intentions of coming down to visit him, Coach Sir pooch raha that tere baare mein. Bola milne tujhse, check how you've been doing. Was asking how are things and what do you plan to do next, I told him, tu toh fatso ho gaya hai, toh coach sir was a bit silent.

With a bit more serious tone, Arvind then asked Jay if he'd ever consider coming back to boxing. At least for the inter-university nationals? Sensing Jay's hesitation in responding to his question, Arvind only said one thing before he took leave. Jay, you can take yourself out of the ring, but can you take the ring out of you? Every fighter dreams of making a comeback irrespective of the years gone by outside of the ring. There's always "One more round" when it comes to life and when it comes to the ring. You just don't give it up like that. And he left.

Late that night, when everything came to a standstill, Jay reflected on his ring buddy and best friends' words – and he did realize that unknowingly the sport had a deep impact on his life, despite, 3 hard hits in life- the loss in the selections despite best possible preparation, failing in HSC despite putting in efforts and rising up to the ultimatum from his family and securing a good rank in the first year of degree, though these series of events had affected him physically and even more when it came to his sanity and his mental health, he had subconsciously been going one more round after the other all thanks to the sport, and with the passage of time had slowly but steadily discovered and created a new version of himself, one that knew which direction required to be taken in which situation, and though he also, he had now, for the first time, in a long time, been able to acknowledge to himself that since the day he had stopped boxing that there was a warrior within who was desperate to make a comeback, and why not, though he had won on all fronts, a victory on this front, in the ring was long overdue, and maybe it was time to go for it.

Part 3. One More Round

Jay was unsure where to begin, he began to spend time back in the sports complex, to get a feel of whether he did really belong in there or had life taken the fighter out of him. He began by spending time observing the new kids who had come in, all this while though there was no talk between his coach, barring a few fleeting visual exchanges at each other.

The calendar was rolled out for the year in mid of July 2003, Boxing was in early August, Jay knew it was now or never, he began roadwork at a nearby open ground after a real long time and could actually feel the difference. While jogging on the second day he thought to himself while out of breath, "So that's how it is after a really long layoff" when he felt a sharp stab of pain in the right side of his lower back and his knees gave way. No matter how hard he tried, just couldn't get up, a good 20 minutes later he managed to drag himself to a bench besides a small temple adjacent to the ground. He knew cycling all the way back to his home was not a possibility, so he called two of his friends, one to drive him back home and the other to fetch his bicycle back home.

Seeing his son in a track suit, perspiring and struggling to walk, Jay's father knew something was wrong, and he also knew what was the reason behind the injury. All he said to his son was, I think we need to take you to a hospital.

X-rays revealed a herniated disc, the doctor advised painkillers and bed rest for a good 15-plus days. Back home Jay's thoughts were troubled, already begun with really less time and now this setback is set to kill most of what was left, he was already feeling demoralized and was contemplating whether to go participate or not, when he realized that it was all up to him, and his mind, and which emotion was strong – the pain or the will to get back in the ring, perhaps for the last time and perhaps, the last opportunity to try for the nationals. Having realized this, he knew what was to be done next.

Though he struggled to, Jay got on his feet, took a hard look at himself, both in the mirror and on the scale, the mirror told an exaggerated truth because body composition can be changed (even a few hours before on the day of the match), but the scale told an even harsher reality, his weight had spiked up to 88 kgs from the 79 kgs during his time away from the sport. This told him that he had graduated weight class and now was a heavyweight (and not a light heavy), he was going in against the biggies (since heavyweight is considered to be a slugfest) and considerable efforts were going to be required.

But hey, look at this Jay thought to himself with the old wry smile, this time, it will be a power game. Trade punches and may the best slugger stand.

Barely 8 days left to go, Jay upped the painkillers and began roadwork, where he could do 8 kilometers in a single go, he saw the difference as he could only go 2, "Push on" he reminded himself at every step of the way.

The day before the bout, he had travelled with Milind (aka Tillu) one of his old friends and now a participant in the fly weight category to the venue that was around 150 kilometres/93 miles away from his hometown. Milind had two more brothers in the state police and he had participated to get one more certificate and try his luck to get in the police basis this certificate.

They reached the venue; and from the looks of it, it was apparent that a lot more were expected to arrive early in the morning. Jay had already stopped eating till weigh in the next day so that he would be light on the stomach and a bit lighter on the scale too. That night those that had arrived sat by a small fire outside, mostly silent as everybody's thoughts were on the next day. Jay went for an early night and woke up early in the morning before sunrise, he wanted to have a look at the participants in the heavy weight category.

Morning dawned, participants poured in, there were almost a 100 plus of them all in various categories, but when it came to the higher weight categories, number lessened which told Jay that there was considerably less competition in the light heavyweight and above categories – a good sign considering the shape he was in, the lesser the better.

Weigh in told him that luck was on his side, there was only 1 other competitors in his weight class, a barely 4' 5" and stout guy, who also had the guts to walk up to Jay and try and psych him out. Jay pretending to be psyched out, let this guy have his fun. "Come in the ring" he thought to himself, this one was going to be a walk in the park.

The bouts began, thudding sounds and audience shouts began in full flow. Since there was no participant in the super heavy weight category, the heavy weight was the last category and was scheduled slight late in the afternoon.

Once again, after a long time, as his bout drew near, Jay, with the eagerness of a child but with the wisdom of Zen went about warming up and preparing for his bout. Systematically he donned on the red corner kit – a coincidence he told himself, it was the same corner colour that he had faced defeat in the last outing. Not this time though, he said to himself as he repeated the drill - the red kit along with red coloured boxing shoes, Jay removed his track suit, put on his inner wraps, gloves, headgear and the gum shield all in a clinical manner.

As he walked toward the ring, he smiled remembering the incident from the day, the 4 feet "Champ" but the change was though he smiled, this time, he was not the same over confident Jay, instead a more mentally sharp, careful person who was at peace irrespective of what the results would be.

As he climbed in the ring, he couldn't see his opponent as the referee was standing in between, he looked at his cornerman Milind and as he noticed the ref moving from the corner of his eye, he saw someone else – a 6' 2" tall bison of a player, surprised, he turned to Milind and said:

It seems I stepped in the wrong ring!!...

Milind responded to him, shoving the gumshield in Jay's mouth:

That's your surprise kid, he had come in asking about you in the afternoon whilst you were busy playing around showing yourself as "psyched out" to the other guy. Now let's see if you can go one more round.

Jay realized that he had been pranked, at a totally different level, but in a split second, as he turned to face his opponent, he said to himself – One more round as the bell rang.

Author- Vinay Kulkarni

Vinay Kulkarni is a Lawyer by passion and is a Lean Six Sigma Green Belt certified professional, certified domain trainer with 13+ years of hands-on experience in Sourcing & Procurement Operations in the shared services industry by profession.

Whilst achieving professional milestones, Vinay, developed a keen interest in writing as a therapy, and being a Co-Founder of WeTalk Literary Agency, Vinay intends to share his bit via the anthology "You are not your mental health".

Vinay Kulkarni is also the founder of WeTalk Legal Rights, an initiative via which he and his team intend to spread legal awareness, provide legal remedies to those who need it the most but cannot afford it, whilst trying to create a useful platform for young minds.

CHAPTER SEVEN

Believe I Can, Watch Me Prosper

Parenting a teenager was growing into a testing task for Mira. Mira could sense that something was wrong with her daughter, Riddhi. Mira noticed that with every passing year, her fun-loving, jovial, bubbly child had started staying in her own shell. Her academics were suffering too. More than her academic performance, Mira was concerned about her sudden transformation into an introvert. There's nothing wrong in being introverted. However, her behavior portrayed that she was supposedly burying some constantly disturbing thoughts or worries within her. That was extremely unhealthy, Mira felt. Riddhi had started distancing herself from her friends, socializing less, never confiding her worries and emotions to even her mother. Earlier, the leisure hours used to be full of her giggles and vibrant laughter. But, now it involved staying in her room and scribbling something into her art book, or lying on the sofa, listlessly watching the cartoon shows on the 40-inch TV, placed in the drawing room.

14-year-old Riddhi returned home exhausted. Mira, her mother, thought that this exertion was an outcome of the rigorous match Riddhi played that day. This was the third time in a row that Riddhi had lost in the badminton match. Her low self-esteem was quite evident this time. As her mother fed her the Dosa, she gently caressed Riddhi's head and whispered, "It's all right. Don't be sad. Practice well next time. Why are you spoiling your mood for this? It happens in sports sweetie!" Her mother's gentle touch and affirmation calmed her nerves for a while. The clock struck 8. Riddhi was busy with her art book. The doorbell rang at 9 PM sharp. It was the time when her father Rishabh returned home from work. As soon as Riddhi spotted Rishabh at the door, she swiftly carried all her art accessories and rushed to her room. This behavior has been quite a common scene now.

Riddhi and Rishabh lived alone in their 2 BHK flat in Nagpur. Rishabh worked as an Engineer in a reputed firm and had shifted here from his hometown, Bareily, 4 years back. Rishabh had sky-high expectations from his daughter. He wanted his girl to be an all-rounder, excelling in all spheres. Being an ambitious, workaholic person, Rishabh hardly had time for his family. Riddhi had got used to her father's emotional unavailability now. It was the dinner time. Mira knew Riddhi was in a bad mood. To bring her frolic back, Mira had prepared Riddhi's favorite, *Chhole Bhature* . As they started the dinner, after shuffling through the news channels for few minutes, Rishabh turned to Riddhi and asked, "So, how was your match?"

Riddhi was pacified that at least he remembers about her match, which he never attended. Riddhi answered quite abruptly, "I lost the match." To which she got the usual reply, "Not again! You are so inattentive. You have to win the next match, else leave the game."

Mira confronted, "Rishabh, it is just a match. Don't create this pressure on her."

Rishabh disliked any other voice interrupting his dominance. He reverted, "Look at your neighbor's daughter, Ruchi. Excellent in academics, super confident speaker, proficient in music! Mr. Sharma carries a pride in his gait. Did you notice? And Riddhi! Scoring 80% seems a mammoth task for her. She was playing well, but now what! Loser, that's what the world will call her. I feel like avoiding everyone who comes my way."

"Rishabh, please calm down! She is just 14. She is your own child. Look, how you're talking to her! Your expectations are creating unrealistic pressure on her. Can't you see that?"

Mira said pointing towards Riddhi, who sat on one corner of the sofa and wept inconsolably. Despair screamed aloud from every inch of her countenance. She was trembling due to the profound yelling going on between her parents.

Rishabh said, "You have pampered her to this extent. She is an Engineer's daughter. A Gold Medalist's daughter! Neither strong academically, nor in any other field. What will she do in life?"

This was not the first time Rishabh was harsh in showing Riddhi her shortcomings. The past four-five years have been the same. The days she tasted success were rejoiced, but, not as much as Riddhi expected on her way back home. When she achieved good yield of her hard work, she received a precious gift and a smile from her father at the end of the day. The days her hard work didn't yield good results, were filled with hours of yelling, scolding, blaming and a lot of it.

The undue pressure, the frustration, the dwindling self-esteem creeping into an innocent child was the reason for her shift from a lively child to an overtly introverted one. It was the pressure produced out of sky-high expectations, a deep-rooted comparison.

Riddhi was hurt badly, she fled to her room and hugged her teddy bear and wept her heart out. The frustration of losing in her attempts yelled aloud. But, more than the dejection, she was hurt to see that her achievements could only be the foundation to receive her father's love. Every morning, her heart pinched to see some of her friends, hugging their fathers as they dropped the kids to school. On the annual day, when all the parents thronged the auditorium, busy clicking pictures of their ward's performance, she could see only her mother in the audience clapping for her, as she concluded her speech in her stammering voice. She never saw her father being present on her special days. The days she played the matches, it was her mother cheering aloud for Riddhi. Her eyes kept searching for her father. And today, when she lost the match, she thought no matter how much the other kids bully her, ridicule her, no matter how much disgust her coach expresses, she will receive some support from her family, particularly her father. She was unaware that such derogatory remarks, such demoralizing rebuke awaited her.

A week later...

It was the usual Sunday morning. Mira was busy preparing her Sunday special breakfast. Riddhi had not stepped out of her room yet. Mira sneaked into her room to check. Riddhi was busy with her art book. Mira heaved a sigh of relief as her anxiety was calming down, seeing Riddhi painting. She rushed to the kitchen to plate up the delicious dosa. It was a cloudy day. The gentle, cold breeze gleefully entered swaying across the flinging curtains. Some white drawing sheets flew away and scattered around the house as the gust of wind swooped across the floor, on which Riddhi sat while painting her emotions on the art sheets. Mira stopped plating the food and stooped down to pick up the sheet that had settled underneath the dining table. The painting struck Mira's heart. The painting had achiever kids being showered with love from their parents and a kid, average performer in academics, being ridiculed by peers and her parents. The message was loud and clear. The pain, the demoralized state of mind that Riddhi was going through, got a clear depiction through art. Mira scuffled randomly through all the paintings that Riddhi had been making for the stretch of her days of a gradual zoning out.

Riddhi stood blank on one corner of the hall gaping at the sorry state of affairs brimming up. Mira rushed with the paintings to Rishabh. "Just look at these, Rishabh! Riddhi is suffering silently. What's her fault, if she is facing difficulty in coping up with the academic pressure?"

Rishabh surfed curiously through the paintings Mira handed him over. Turning the sheets one after another, left Rishabh in shock. His expression spoke the heart of a father overflowing with grief. Few sheets depicted the sketch of a teenage girl being bullied for being a mediocre performer. Some showed a teenage girl with a winning expression and a crowd clapping for her on one end and another teenager with a dejected face and extremely lonely. The last one caused Rishabh a tear, crawling past his face that dropped on the black colour predominating the painting, smudging it off. It was again of a teenage girl with a hairstyle akin to Riddhi's. This subject of Riddhi's painting was clouded in a dark cloud of despair, with a thinking cloud on the top left. The cloud read, "I am no one. I am an under achiever. I don't deserve love from Mom and Dad. I hope I don't have to see the shame on Dad's face."

Rishabh was shocked. Remorse and guilt filled his soul. Mira charged Rishabh for this situation. They were unable to find a way to help their daughter. Riddhi felt unloved and internally blamed her grades and declining performance in sports for this feeling. Riddhi was battling a tough fight between her heart and mind. HEART, that yearned for her father's love, irrespective of her success or failure! MIND, which was constantly running a race to prove its worth, regardless of her intrinsic desires! A desire to find her inner calling, a desire to figure out her strength, a desire to discover faith in her parents' eyes! It was a sensitive tug of war, with HEART and MIND at its two ends.

A constant dilemma reigned over her innocent heart. "I am incapable." "I don't deserve love." "I am a loser."

Like most of the other days, she restricted herself to her room, in her snail-like protective shield, a shield fencing her against those judgmental eyes.

Rishabh, on the other hand, was filled with guilt, a realization that was breaking his heart into a thousand pieces. His only intent towards his strict composure was to raise Riddhi into an achiever. He intended to train her to work hard. He wanted his daughter to be ready to face challenges and secure a foothold in the competitive world. The negative impact it had created on his child never caught his attention. He felt he had got detached from his daughter emotionally, while imposing his sky-high expectations on her. Mira was worried about Riddhi. She was anxious about finding a way to help her child, to help her know that they love her. But, probably it was difficult to convince her now. She freaked out. She confronted Rishabh strongly today.

"Rishabh, our little child is heartbroken! She feels we don't love her!", Mira was furious as tears rolled down her eyes. She was unable to see her daughter suffering silently.

"Rishabh, do you even know about her likes and dislikes? You kept on blaming her, scolding her, demoralizing her. Did you ever bother to spend time with her? Did you ever express your love for her?"

Rishabh was silent. He was shattered today. He was cribbing himself for having failed to assure his child that her father loves her. Mira dragged Rishabh towards Riddhi's room. They stood at the door and Mira showed him her wilting state of mind. Riddhi lay on her bed, staring at the stars on the ceiling of her room, hugging her teddy. She had a blank look with distaste towards expressing verbally what she was feeling within.

"It's 10 PM and Riddhi has not eaten a morsel of food since morning. I tried to feed her, but she resisted. There is something going on inside her. Look, what you have turned my bubbly child into! I am concerned about her health and her feelings. You go and run after what our neighbor's child achieved today." Mira walked away in sheer disgust.

The plight of watching his teenage daughter in such a disturbed state of mind shook Rishabh's conscience. Self-condemnation was enough to have channelized his thought process in the other direction. He decided to take the first step to correct his flaws. He rushed to the dining area, plated up the food and rushed straight to Riddhi's room. Riddhi was facing the other side. Rishabh sat beside her gently and caressed her head softly. There was silence. He caressed her and asked, "You haven't eaten anything!" Riddhi sat up, still looking the other way.

"I am sorry I couldn't understand my words were hurting you. I didn't realize I was creating an unbearable stress on you. I am sorry I kept imposing what I wanted you to do and never asked what you wished." Rishabh's voice was turning husky. Riddhi broke her silence for the first time. "Dad, I am sorry you feel ashamed as I am a failure. I am incapable."

Rishabh replied in a way that was beyond Riddhi's understanding. "So, if you are saying you failed to achieve well in sports and academics, I failed too! I failed as a father! I failed in letting you feel loved. I am a bigger failure. Can we solve this issue together? Can we please help each other? Today, I am all ears. Tell me what you love doing the most! Tell me about your aptitude today!"

Riddhi was still trying to analyze this abrupt change in her father's attitude. Something clicked her instantly and she jumped forward to hug her father. "Dad, would you still love me if I lose in the badminton match sometimes?"

" Forgive me, my child that this question could crop up in your mind. I love you, Mom loves you too. Our entire family loves you. Let's help each other. I and your Mom will be there beside you, regardless of failures, moments of success." Riddhi hugged her father just like a newborn baby. She could feel that she has got her father back. She could feel guilt racing across his nerves.

"Can we have some food?" uttered Riddhi, to which a smiling Rishabh nodded a big yes. He picked up the plate full of food and fed his daughter. Mira, who was silently watching everything from the door, couldn't resist. She joined the long-awaited family moment. The night continued with lots of serious talks, tears, smiles and detangled loops of resentment, grudges and misinterpretations.

Children expect love, lots of care and affection. They also need belief and faith. They need the canopy of parental support. They need motivating guidance. Imposing expectations robs them of their self-esteem. Efforts dilute from their side and the willingness to dream extinguishes. Riddhi needed a lot of time to rebuild her self-confidence. But, at least, she was happy that her parents love her. And this love would gradually heal the invisible wounds, the pain, and the scars her little heart had housed for so long! Scars of being stranded alone!

Author- Pallabi Ghoshal

Pallabi Ghoshal is a versatile wordsmith and a passionate storyteller from Kolkata. She is the author of the published books, THE QUEST OF VERMILLION and AN

UNEXPECTED DETOUR. She has co-authored with an eminent author in a poetry anthology titled MY LIFE IN POEMS. Poignant tales of love and loss, stories of resilience and utmost strength, or the world of some compelling mysteries that keep you on a cliffhanger, Pallabi's stories have touched the hearts of readers. Pallabi hails from Kolkata. She started writing at the age of 12 and has contributed stories in 14 anthologies as well. She runs her own blogs across Wordpress, Medium and Substack.

CHAPTER EIGHT

The Bougainvillea

Tojo stands near the dining hall, with folded hands, rubbing her feet, one against the other, bowing her head. Her eyes, oozing involuntary saline droplets, falling directly on her feet, wetting them and her slippers, continuously. Baba has strict instructions for Ma, "do not serve her dinner". Tojo has been asked to stand there and watch everyone eat. She does not look up but can hear her family having dinner along with the relatives, the sounds of food can be so torturous, so insulting, she had no clue earlier. She's hungry and nauseous. Can a sorrowful soul really gulp in food? She ponders, but her stomach hurts. Why is Baba being so cruel? Is it a crime to watch a cartoon show, that too on a Sunday? all her friends do. Other days Baba fastens the shutters of their box television with its inbuilt lock and takes the key to the bazaar, he taps his pocket rechecking them before leaving the house. This morning, he somehow misses locking it, in a hurry. Relatives have poured in last night. Tojo takes the liberty to watch her favourite program, the Mickey and Donald show at nine in the morning, airing on Doordarshan. Her cousins insist her to switch on the television, she sits along with them. She is expected to sit somewhere else and study, instead. Is it just discipline or does Baba derives some kind of pleasure tormenting her? Has he changed over these years or did she not recognise him earlier? If growing up is so painful, why doesn't she just cease to, Tojo thinks in silence. Why couldn't she perish in the womb? She feels like Uncle Tom trapped in his cabin forever.

Swajal Sanyal, the fourth kid of the family who is being raised in an orphanage along with his siblings, knows food as just a lump of green boiled and mashed vegetables with thick sticky rice, provided in missionaries. Salt brings some taste to the bland food. Honestly, the immense hunger eradicates the need for quality and emphasises on the quantity mostly, the taste becomes irrelevant.

The warden keeps a series of long, hard, brown cane sticks, oiled and polished, using them against children who go astray. The little skinny bodies bend over and the oily cane comes on their backs over and over again, repeatedly, till the breaking point, either for the kids or the cane. There is no place to run to, no one to complain to. No one, to say a word or two of compassion or apply ointment over their wounds. None to ask what they want for birthdays, Durga puja or Christmas. Half of them don't even know what a birthday is, most of them are without any.

Losing their father at the age of two, Swajal only knows his mother, who suddenly from The Sanyal Ginni-ma (the Sanyal landlady), metamorphoses to a helpless lady clad in old faded and torn saris, shifting from different relatives' house for shelter with her five children. When everyone starts reasoning the adversity of keeping six extra members in a single household, she decides to send her children to different orphanages, herself working all day at her sister's house. She hopes, someday, when her kids grow up to be adults, she can live with them under the same roof. Build a house of their own, like before, call it theirs.

Amidst all the days of hunger, hammering of canes and missing his mother's palm across his warm forehead during soaring body temperatures, Swajal grows up along with others in the orphanage including his siblings. He grows up fighting temptations of owning a piece of land and a house in exchange of conversions of faith. He begins a journey to dream of building a house himself someday, where he can lie down resting his head on his mother's lap, with all his siblings on the jute mat on a moon-lit terrace. They would recall the days of going through emotional rollercoaster with their mother sitting near all of them, sharing each one's experiences of all the years of ordeal with puffed rice indulged in mustard oil and green chillies, a single bowl and six hands. Where food will be just sufficient and will come without rebukes.

By the time, Swajal completes his degrees for a job, his mother is long gone by then, taking her two sons along with her, succumbing to tuberculosis. He sits near the ghats of Ganga, looking at his empty palms, listening to the unceasing splashes of the muddy waters near the mossy steps of the Ghat. The October wind sending chills over his head, shaved clean after the rituals of last rites of his elder brother. He looks at the setting sun beyond the silhouettes of dark trees and hedges on the other side of the bank. Far away, someone plays raga Jaijaivanti on a sarod, he cannot get the entirety of it. As if, it is the background score of all his pain, faintly mellowing the evening with heaviness. He witnesses another Apurba Kumar Ray of Pather Panchali, in himself, barren, lost and lonely. Ganga changes to Icchamoti in front of his eyes, he visualises his Ma's faded and torn sari afloat in the gloomy waters, he is trying to get hold of it, struggling to gather it, with all the strength he is left with but fails. This evening, as he stands with his dhoti half submerged in the river water, the setting day devours a piece of his soul and sinks beyond the saffron waters.

Five years later, when he meets Shambhobi, in a family gathering, her doe eyes install hope in his pounding heart. She lost her mother at a very early age, raised in a joint family where her father, grandma, uncles and aunts ran the household. Nineteen-year-old Shambhobi decides on a twenty-seven-year-old Swajal and immediately they propose on settling down. Though her father wanted Shambhobi to complete her masters, but she declines. She has to build a new life with this man whose barrenness she has to flourish with love and fulfillment. She flows in like a river over the parched land that lay lifeless for years. Love blooms, harvesting prosperity, the dry land changes to lush deep greenery.

Tejeshwini, a thirteen-year-old Tojo, can't see anything beyond her father. He is everything to her. Her hero. The most honest, good-looking, epitome of justice, her father. Things start getting messed up with the onset of her father's ruined business, and the toll starts showing in his behaviour. Financial stability crumbles, devouring everything happy in the Sanyal household. School fees, starts getting delayed, barring her from terminal examinations. She stands in the scorching heat of March, in Kolkata, along with other defaulters, seeing her classmates writing their papers, asking for extra sheets. A tearful Tojo, faces the humiliation till the last hour when she's allowed to sit to write her examination. Progress report doesn't look progressive enough, blotched with red numerical everywhere. "Get this signed by your father, understand?", the class teacher scorns. Surely, she predicted the consequences and the series of events anticipating that evening. This is not something that is going to happen for the first time. Their house was filled with perpetual guests throughout the year. They come, feast, sit, laugh and gossip even during examinations. Ma always said, "One who is sincere will make arrangements for their studies, Ishwar Chandra Vidya Sagar learned his lessons under a lamppost, you know". Tojo knows and understands she is not like any stalwart, ma or Baba set examples of. She's a normal human being with limitations, with shortcomings, with faults. People who flock their house, advise her to study well, yet never leave her alone for her lessons. Some even try putting their dirty hands over her tender body, which she can't even confide to her parents, these kinds of things are forbidden for discussion. She feels, they might think its somehow her fault. Her head pulsates, she feels scared, helpless, unsafe in her own house, attacked by people who are known to her.

With a heavy head, she carries the pale green report card to Baba. Tojo travels to the orphanage school of Krishna Nagar as a time traveler, where oily brown canes would crack on the tender skinny backs of homeless kids. She witnesses the happenings like an audience as if watching a movie, her Baba's childhood. The ochre wooden ruler replaces the canes now, at times iron cloth hangers, Baba ties her hands with her skipping rope, so there's no escape. Each time he strikes her, it leaving deep crimson lines on her fair skin, she reminds herself the stories she tells her friends in school about her father. Stories that she makes up, stories where her father dreads the thought of raising his hands on her, where her beloved Baba, fights Ma protecting her. Indulges her tantrums, hugs her to sleep narrating stories. Baba's repeated questions fall flat to her ears, he asks her over and over again, where has he lapsed in providing her a good life to deserve such a report card.

He compares the food and shelter he had with that Tojo has now. She has parents, he didn't. Tojo has developed numbness as a defence mechanism, Baba knows the answer yet is in denial. You are prepared for the blows from unknown people in your life but it's bewildering when you are hurt most by people you know to be your own, you start detesting the place you've learned all these years to be your home, it's now a place where your loved ones scare you. Punches and slaps follow till he gets tired. He gives a task to prepare all the twelve lessons from her history book by dinner, if Tojo wishes to be spared. An entire syllabus of a year, is demanded to be completed in four hours, Tojo knows Baba is asking for the impossible and preparing himself to return with more of his rebukes and physical punishments. The struggle continues without food, till two in the morning. Finally, Ma intervenes, asks Baba to spare Tojo for next day's school. The report card remains unsigned following further humiliations at school. Her classmates' stares at her, when asked for a signed report card.

Parents are called. Ma avoids visiting her school, Baba does. It surprises her to see her father and the class teacher are so cordial to each other, so much on the same page. Her Baba asks her to learn from such a wonderful teacher and her teacher says that she is lucky to have such a father, Tojo listens with her head stooped low, staring at her black school shoes. The report card finally gets her father's initials after two more days, with few extra slaps at school and home.

Tojo feels pushed away from her father each moment, slipping from the most secure place she knew on earth. She slips from his shoulders and keeps falling somewhere dark, unknown, delving into a never-ending pit of loneliness, for reasons she cannot comprehend. She starts believing herself worthless and undeserving of the life she is provided. Listening to her friends at school, talking about their fathers, dotting on them, she makes up stories, similar to theirs, with a lump of lies choking her throat. The more she makes them up the more shameful she feels. She sits near the edge of the terrace of their single-storied house, thinking of possible ways to end this suffering. Baba doesn't even talk to her nicely. She finds it difficult to remember the last time Baba speaking to her, without a pour of scorn. Baba isn't like this with other kids. He showers affection upon the children who come as guests or relatives, he specifies who amongst them will love him the most when he grows old, or who will take care of him when he is unable to do that by himself. He calls them names, special ones given by him out of adoration. He holds their hand, even of the ones elder to Tojo when the families plan an outing together. She watches her Baba's hands are full, she doesn't even have his finger of his to hold on to, so she just follows them. Their parents love them, her Baba loves them. She receives nothing. Why is she left out in this barrenness. It's unfair, it's unfortunate, it's cruel.

Tojo's parents seem to raise their kids to please people around them. As if, this child did not have anything else other than being a trophy to the family, Tojo is definitely not a trophy, she's a shame. The financial difficulties barred them from having new clothes during festivities. Tojo never complains. She understands her father is not being able to provide, its unintentional, she backs out from picnics where contributing is mandatory, she gives up her paid computer classes takes up economics instead but Baba is not as considerate as this thirteen-year-old.

November 26th, Tuesday, the chills post Diwali is gradually setting in. Ma and Baba both are out to attend a relative's sudden demise. "What if Tojo leaves the world today? She thinks in desperation. What can be quick, easy, painless? She tries imagining her parent's faces seeing her lifeless body. She will be far beyond Baba's punches and strikes of the ochre wooden ruler. Teardrops roll out, thinking she would not make it till the coming years of her life. What will happen to all the poems she has written? Baba will surely burn them off, Ma might shed a tear or two. What will they do with her charcoal sketches? She wants Baba to run and come to stop her, hug her for once. She wants him not to call her stupid in-front of all the guests. To hold her hand and say, "I'm sorry, your studies get disrupted for so many guests, I'll take care of it. No one can touch you for as long as I'm alive. I'm sorry, I couldn't pay your fees on time. I'm sorry, for the delay, you had only one hour to write three hours paper. I'm sorry, to have hurt you physically multiple times, knowing well how much it pains".

Tojo, keeps looking at the door, but no one turns up. She opens the drawer where her Baba keeps his shaving tools, she takes out a double-edged blade with her trembling cold hands and walks back to the bathroom. She knows how much it will hurt but it's as clear as day that this will be her last pain. Sweating profusely, she sits near the door, on the floor, knowing well if she thinks too much, she might not be able to do what she has planned. There have been numerous occasions when she has failed, trying hanging herself with the same skipping rope that Baba uses to tie her hands, but the ceiling is so high, she couldn't reach. She used to love to skip and hop with this rope so much sometimes back, but now it's so disdainful, a symbol of torment. Tojo gathers all her strength and courage to bring the blade close to her left wrist, and with one go she slits it letting the unconstrained flow of red liquid run wild drenching her soft peach cotton T-shirt, dripping, crossing her thighs, spreading like a meandering rivulet towards the drainage sewer. Her unwanted self, her less important blood is running free, she feels dizzy with each moment, as though she's growing wings gradually to fly away to some far-off land, free forever. A thick curtain of darkness descends before her eyes and she prepares to sleep in peace forever.

Tojo, wakes up in a hospital bed, blood and saline drip running in her veins through pricking needles. She hears Baba, calling her a coward to give up on life. "How can she be such a weakling?" He doubts that he's her father, a man who didn't lose hope even after losing everything. Ma, asks him to talk softly. Another failure. She doesn't know where will this end and how. Now she has to live with few more feathers to her crown, coward and weakling.

A week later, Tojo is discharged. Dr. Ashit Ghosh advises a strict monitoring along with benevolence. "Teshaswini is a sensitive child, and she needs love and care at home, people who attempt killing oneself generally keep on attempting it multiple times. She needs counselling and I expect, without prejudice Mr. and Mrs. Sanyal will attend the sessions as it is the home atmosphere that needs to be discussed." He says.

"You think we don't love our child? We torture her? We don't provide for her?", Swajal's ice-clad voice rose in defiance.

"You see, Mr. Sanyal, your definition of love might be a little different from what this child requires for a healthy life. I'm sure you love your child, but she needs to live and that too, happily. I need your cooperation, you must not regret your principles sometime in your life in future, let me remind you, Tejaswini might not be able to use her left hand like before for quite a long time, her physical wounds will heal with time, but your love and care can help her recover psychologically.", replied Dr. Ghosh.

Tojo, Tesjaswini Sanyal, 6ᵗʰ standard, didn't get the opportunity to be promoted to class seven. She left, with a heavy heart, that craved for her father's love and attention, finally successful in one of her many experimental attempts. It's been almost thirty years now, Swajal babu sits with Shambhobi Devi in their bedroom, looking at nothingness. All those relatives who loved coming to their house once, doesn't even call them. The people, including adults and children among relatives, whom Swajal babu took so much care to please, not a single soul enquires about their being alive. Shambhobi devi, fumbles old rusty albums looking at yesteryear's monochrome and Polaroid's of Tojo. Photos that still hold on their little moments of togetherness, photos that reminds of her empty womb, her barren life, her home that's just a house now. She can't cook these days; they depend on home delivery food service. Swajal babu's glasses are thick and heavy now. Post cataract, he feels uncomfortable, something might be wrong with the procedure, he thinks. Using the ATM card, withdrawing money, visiting banks are gradually becoming difficult with passing days. The television blares Bengali soap operas twenty-four into seven, no one watches them, except Bashonti, their part-time help. The old box television is replaced with a new one, these days televisions doesn't come with locks. Their enormous house has no heir, its mostly occupied by tenants, it well might go to some charity after they are gone or to his nephew, it's still not decided.

Perhaps, in some other universe, in a different dimension, is Tojo living a different life? Where Baba is her confidant, her strength, where she knows she can tell him anything and everything. Where schools are banned from corporal punishments, from negative reinforcements, public humiliations. Where their house is a home, where she lives with Baba and Ma, laughing, cracking jokes, singing and listening to stories on their moonlit terrace, where her mistakes are discussed, reasoned and solved together. A place where Baba understands the way he was raised was wrong and rectify the paths of upbringing. Where they go for vacations and restrict relatives' visits during examinations. Tejaswini lives a different life there, grows up, falls in love, confides in her parents, succeeds in her career, have babies, takes Baba and Ma for regular trips and medical checkups. Where Swajal babu, boasts about his daughter, sitting with his friends in the park, every morning after walks. Shambhobi devi complains, how her grandchildren are naughty unlike their mother, running after them and feeding them. Tojo's Baba is Dadu now, taking pride in all his grandkids' playfulness. He reads new stories awaiting holidays, preparing himself for them. Stores chocolates and candies in his secret cabinet. His balcony filled with clothesline of miniature soft linen-smelling innocence.

Turning his hunched stature away from Shambhobi and her albums, Swajal babu stands from his chair today. He looks lean and shrunk in his loose pale, off-white pyjama, filling into a half-sleeve ill fitted cotton kurta. Walking with a pace as much as his worn-out body can carry him, to their semi-circular huge balcony in southern Kolkata, facing west. His vision is obscure like the muddy waters of Ganga Ghat, the chill of October wind gives him the shivers. Someone is playing raga Jaijaivanti in the neighbourhood, strangely. Today he is more barren than Apurba Kumar Ray, he revisits the waters of Icchamoti, visualises all the ochre wooden rulers afloat in its sage green moss-filled waters, they have an uncanny resemblance with all the oiled cane sticks of Krishna Nager orphanage, hard, painful and ruthless. Swajal babu, tries to gather them, but they sink one by one, leaving nothing behind, other than foams and bubbling sounds among the ripples of murky waters. Looking beyond the climbers that are filled with dark peach bougainvilleas, he can faintly see the saffron scratches of the setting sun engraved all over the greyish purple sky. The dark outlines of the background is obscure today. He clutches the iron grill, its peeled paint in places, exposed, rusty, pricks his feeble hands, hands whose toughness is replaced with soft, mellow skin, thin and paper like. Hands showing green veins carrying the same blood that was seeping each day from someone else's tattered arteries years back.

Teardrops roll down his soft wrinkled unshaven face, more follow, blurring his pre-existing faded vision, making it a little more hazed. He sighs, bowing his tired head, with only one name in mind, "Tojo".

Author- Sudeshna Das Chakravarty

Sudeshna Das Chakravarty, originally from Kolkata, presently settled in Guwahati, is a motivational speaker and a councellor by profession. Her passion takes wonderful forms in her writing, sketches and delectable food. This storyteller often finds herself in photography clubs and theatre.

CHAPTER NINE

2020, Truly Unforgettable!

It was the start of 2020, and the new year brought with it the joy of having my in-laws visit us for three months. Their visa was set to expire in March, but considering the spread of Covid, we decided to book their tickets early. Since the kids' school was closing for a short break, we decided to send them to India with their grandparents.

We thought it would be wonderful for the kids to spend some quality time with my brother-in-law and his little ones in Bangalore. Especially since my wife had been looking forward to a week-long vacation in April, it seemed like the perfect opportunity for the children to bond and create lasting memories together. She intended to bring them back when she returned. On March 11th, the day finally arrived for my in-laws to depart, taking our kids with them. It was a tough moment at the airport, a wave of emotions washed over us. It was hard to see them go, but we knew they'd have a great time in India. Even though it is just a matter of three weeks, we knew we would miss them dearly.

I had been working with one of the top companies in the UAE for 12 years, and it felt like a second home to me. This organization was not just where I worked; it was where I found my passion, where I grew both personally and professionally. Every day felt like a part of a bigger family, and I couldn't have imagined a better place to invest my time and energy. The company was doing well, with good business turnover and a sense of stability in the workplace. However, everything changed suddenly one evening in the middle of March. We were all informed to leave the office without any prior notice. It felt like a punch to the gut, leaving us all reeling in shock and disbelief. We hoped it was just a temporary setback, perhaps due to some internal management issues that would be fixed soon.

As the Covid-19 outbreak unfolded, masks and social distancing became a must. At the same time, my father's health was worsening, and it made me anxious. We found out late that he had cancer, and it had already progressed to the fourth and final stage. By the end of March, the COVID-19 virus had spread, and the country's airports shut down for 14 days. I was eager to visit my father and had plans to fly out as soon as the airport reopened. My wife had already booked tickets to Bangalore and was excited about seeing my kids. But then we heard that the airports would only open when the Covid situation improves.

As the days stretched into weeks with no news from the office, the uncertainty pressed down on us like a heavy blanket. The entire staff was getting nervous, but we held onto the confidence that the company would open soon. In the midst of this waiting game, there was a silver lining - my father's health started improving. He began talking with us more, and it brought a sense of relief. However, in Bangalore, my mother-in-law faced challenges getting the kids to sleep at night. They would cry and ask for my wife. It was the first time they had stayed without us for so many days.

In a few days, my father's health further deteriorated, and traveling was out of the question. I kept calling my sister to get updates on his condition. On May 3rd afternoon, my father was rushed to the hospital. When I spoke to my mother, she was completely drained. I felt so powerless sitting in Dubai, unable to be by their side. Then, at midnight, my phone rang. It was my brother-in-law. As I answered confidently, I could hear the pain in his voice as he said, "Father left us, brother, father left us." I was speechless and trembling with shock. It was so hard to believe. We never imagined he would leave us so soon. In the next minute, I called all my cousins and informed them, and asked them to quickly coordinate with my sister and brother-in-law. I couldn't attend the final rituals and pay my respects in person. Instead, I had to watch the cremation through a video conference. It felt heartbreaking not being able to be there with my loved ones during such a difficult time. I couldn't help but curse the pandemic and the circumstances that kept us apart. It's moments like these that remind us of the harsh realities of the world we are living in.

As COVID cases continued to rise and more restrictions were put in place, I was slowly starting to feel better after dealing with so much trauma. Then one morning, as I woke up, I realized something was seriously wrong – I couldn't lift my right hand properly. It was like it had lost all its strength, and I could only move it a little bit. I was terrified, so I called my wife right away. She tried everything she could think of, from putting balm on it to giving me hot massage therapy, but nothing seemed to make a difference. The following week, things got even worse. I woke up one day and found that I couldn't stand up properly because of the intense pain on the right side of my lower back. It was agonizing, and I couldn't do anything without leaning on something for support. Now it was like half of my body was paralyzed. It was June, and my office still hadn't reopened. With airports still closed, my kids remained separated from us. Along with dealing with my dad's passing and my declining health, I felt really down. It was like everything was happening at once, weighing me down more and more each day. My wife was slipping into depression, worried about kids. It felt like a never-ending cycle of challenges, leaving us both feeling helpless and overwhelmed.

Despite facing so many challenges, we decided to focus on what we could control. It was tough, but we knew we had to keep pushing forward. One thing that really kept us going was the amazing support from our friends. They stood by us through it all, offering their help and encouragement whenever we needed it. I started exploring Ayurveda treatment for my health issues, while my wife dove into joining social media and WhatsApp groups. She worked tirelessly to bring our kids back from India, where they had been stranded due to the airport closures. It was a difficult time for many families in similar situations, but we all came together and fought for a solution. We joined forces with other families and children facing similar challenges, and together we worked towards getting emergency flights arranged to the UAE. It was a long and difficult process, but finally, in August, our prayers were answered. Our hard work paid off, and our kids were finally reunited with us.

In November, when the airport finally opened up, I flew back to India, my hometown. The moment I arrived, I could see my mom eagerly waiting for me, her eyes filled with tears as she looked at my father's photo. I wasn't able to get close or give my mom a hug due to social distancing measures. She cried loudly as if a huge wave of relief washed over her upon seeing me. Witnessing her emotional reaction brought tears to my eyes, and those moments are still etched in my memory, making me emotional whenever I think about them. Upon arrival, I had to undergo a mandatory seven-day quarantine, during which I was tested for COVID-19. Thankfully, the result came back negative, allowing me to finally embrace my mother after such a long separation.

However, my health journey wasn't over yet. I spent three weeks at an Ayurveda hospital, undergoing complete therapy to address my health issues. Day by day, I could feel myself slowly getting better, until finally, on the 16th day, I had completely recovered. It was a joyous moment when I realized I could lift my hand and walk without any support, just like before. I owe a huge debt of gratitude to the doctor and therapist who worked tirelessly to help me regain my health. Their dedication and expertise played a crucial role in my recovery, and I will always be thankful for their support during such a challenging time.

When I returned to Dubai at the end of December, little did I know that it was the beginning of a transformative journey. Despite the uncertainty of my job's delay, I chose to see it as an opportunity for growth and exploration. I immersed myself in activities that fueled my soul – reading, writing, gardening, and cooking. Each day became a canvas for creativity, a chance to delve deeper into my passions and discover new ones. As I dedicated myself to learning and self-improvement, I found solace in my YouTube channel. With every video I produced, I poured my heart into it – scripting, presenting, editing – every step was a labor of love. Months passed in a blur of activity, and

I found myself fully engaged in my new ventures. From launching my own blog to contributing articles to magazines, I was on fire with passion and purpose.

But beyond the accolades and achievements, what truly resonated with me was the realization that my journey could inspire others. Through my words and videos, I aimed to ignite a spark of hope and determination in anyone facing uncertainty or adversity. Life may not always unfold as we expect, but it's in those unexpected moments that we discover our true strength and purpose. So embrace the journey, trust in the process, and never underestimate the power of pursuing your passions with unwavering dedication.

Author- Arun P T

Meet PTee, a passionate writer, storyteller and content creator known for crafting engaging blogs and captivating videos. PTee enjoys hosting interactive workshops for children, where he encourages creativity and sparks their curiosity. Beyond the screen, he devotes time to volunteering, embodying values of compassion and respect in every interaction. Inspired by Maya Angelou's words, he strives to be a rainbow in someone's cloud, spreading joy and positivity wherever he goes. With a heart dedicated to making a difference, PTee continues to weave narratives that inspire, uplift, and connect people from all walks of life. He is supported by a loving wife and two children, mother is his inspiration and friends are his pillars of strength.

CHAPTER TEN

Down the Memory Lane

It has been raining heavily since the morning. Dr. Deepa thought that none of her patients would come today for therapy. Deepa is a psychologist aged 28. She has a small oval-shaped face and a mesmerizing smile. She had been practicing for only two years.

While Deepa checked the previous patient's history her assistant came into the room.

"Madam, a patient has come but she doesn't have any appointment for today. Do you want to meet her?" The assistant asked Deepa with confusion in her eyes.

"Because of the rain no other patient has come, you can let her in," Deepa said and nodded her head in affirmation.

A few minutes later a girl came into Deepa's room. The girl had long curly blue hair and a round face. Her hand was covered with different tattoos.

"Please sit", Deepa showed the chair in front of the desk.

The girl sat on the chair, her face was looking frightened and her whole body was shivering.

Deepa thought that if anything she asked the girl now might make her situation worse so instead of asking anything she thought that she would start practicing breathing exercises with the girl.

"Hey, could you please try to take some deep breaths with me?" Deepa said looking into the girl's eyes.

The girl who wasn't even looking nodded her head politely.

"Inhale and exhale," Deepa said.

After a few minutes when Deepa felt that the girl was in a stable condition, she started asking basic questions. She learned that the girl's name is Sudeshna, and she is in her fourth year of studying engineering.

****

"So since when are you doing this deliberate self-harm?" Deepa asked in a concerned manner after having a few conversations.

"I don't remember actually," The girl said while scratching her head.

"Okay. What do you think why you want to do it?" Deepa asked with a voice like a dove.

"I feel it makes me feel better, I remember the first time I did it when I was maybe around thirteen or fourteen years old," The girl said as she started feeling comfortable with Deepa.

"Can you remember what the reason was when the first time you did self-harm?" Deepa asked and looked at her hand which was full of scars.

"Well," Sudeshna took a deep breath and started telling the story from five years ago.

"My mum and dad got divorced when I was just six years old. My dad used to meet me every Friday. I used to wait the whole week for Friday as my dad was my favorite person. My mother always used to say curse words towards him, she used to say that my dad left us for another woman, but I never trusted her, my dad used to be the best as I used to feel. But then one day while I was returning from school along with my friends, I saw my dad with another woman, and he was carrying a boy kid in his arms. I came home and locked my room. I took my mum's lighter and burned a small portion of skin in one of my legs." Sudeshna sighed.

Deepa suddenly started feeling hollow in her heart as the story was making her remember a lot of things from her traumas. She ignored her own feelings and asked...

"How did you feel that time? Before you burn your skin?"

"Betrayed, angry," Sudeshna said as tears started dropping from her eyes.

"You know not all the times I feel like this, there have been months maybe I felt extremely happy and energetic, and then again, I feel very depressed and It's very hard to move from the bed. One of the doctors said I tend to be bipolar. I was feeling very suicidal, and I didn't get any appointment of his, so I searched on Google and came to know about your place."

"Okay....So, when you feel stressed how do you cope with it?" Deepa asked with empathy in her voice.

"Well, I never thought about it. I only try to be dependent on medicines" Sudeshna replied.

"What you do is right, but you also must learn some strategies to cope with your high and low moods. Could you please write down your emotions in this diary?" Deepa handed over a new diary from her desk to Sudeshna.

"I am feeling Suicidal," Sudeshna said without even looking at the diary.

"Okay... tell me what is coming into your mind?" Deepa asked while she noticed that Deepa herself had started sweating.

"I want to end my life; my life has no meaning..."

****

After the therapy session was over Deepa went to the washroom and looked at the mirror. She could see a boy from six years ago, begging for help. Deepa understood that she had started hallucinating again. Deepa started splashing water on her face and every time she closed her eyes, she could see a never-ending staircase. Somehow, she managed to get out of the washroom, and she went to her house.

****

"Hey, you are late. I made chai. Want to have?" Deepa's boyfriend Nikhil asked as soon as she reached home.

Deepa started sharing her flat with Nikhil two months ago, she felt she had moved on from that incident but today again she felt the same as five years ago.

"I want some rest," Deepa said and went into her room.

Five Years Ago

Deepa was doing her master's in psychology from Mumbai. That day Deepa had two classes early in the morning. After the class ended, she went to the canteen to have some breakfast, as she was late for college, she didn't get any time to fill my stomach with anything. That time it was raining heavily. She ordered a cup of cappuccino and one soupy Maggie. She took the food and sat at the corner table. She started having the cappuccino while reading a book.

"Deepa, Kartik ...." Avishek screamed. Avishek was Deepa's best friend in college, he was in the physics department. He had a long face, wearing a blue t-shirt with ripped jeans.

The cappuccino tipped over from Deepa's hand and all its contents had fallen on her lap.

Though she could feel the burning sensation she didn't care, she felt something was wrong, maybe something terrible had happened to Kartik.

"Kartik had fallen while doing some experiment in the lab, he was having seizures, and he collapsed on the ground" Avishek was breathing heavily.

The moment she heard this she felt as if someone had snatched everything from her, her mind wasn't able to understand how to react.

Without even thinking about anything from the past or for the future she ran towards the chemistry department. The department was almost a kilometer away from the canteen, so she ran without thinking about anything. Her skirt blew from the wind, and she ran as the current flowed into the river.

After reaching the department's building she paused for a second and took a deep breath. The lab was on the third floor, and without even thinking to get up in the elevator She started climbing the stairs, she felt as if it was a never-ending path, and her heart started beating faster as she completed each floor. The moment She reached the entrance of the Lab She felt my heart had stopped, Kartik was there on a chair, someone was holding his head as he couldn't hold his head straight anymore, and his lips had turned blue, and his pupils were looking different.

"The ambulance has come, hold him, everyone," The lab assistant told the other students.

She stood at the entrance like a stone, her head was blank as if there was nothing left in this whole universe. They somehow managed to lift Kartik's unconscious body and took him towards the elevator.

"Deepa, are you okay?" Avishek asked her empathetically.

At that moment Deepa wasn't there anymore, she couldn't hear anything.

"Deepa, hey Deepa" Avishek shook her by the shoulder.

"Yeah," Deepa said as if suddenly she woke from a nightmare.

"What happened to him?" Deepa looked at Avishek in confusion.

"No one knows, let's go to the hospital together."

"Avishek, is he going to die?" Deepa said the thing she feared the most.

"Shhh......" Avishek hushed me and hugged her.

The Ambulance arrived before we reached, and the doctors admitted Kartik to the ICU. They said that it looked like a case of poisoning. There were five more classmates of Kartik and one professor who went to the hospital. Deepa and Avishek were standing outside the ICU and the classmates of Kartik were all together standing a little away from us. Suddenly Deepa could hear their whispers.

"I think Kartik tried committing suicide," A boy said to the other classmates.

"Of course, he has. Otherwise, how can he be poisoned in the chemistry lab, maybe he has taken it from the lab only." One girl said.

"But why? Was there any girl?"

Deepa looked at Avishek and couldn't hold herself anymore. She started sobbing heavily.

"Hey, hey it's okay, he will be alright," Avishek said with empathy in his voice.

"It's all my fault. Kartik called me this morning and I ignored it. He told me everything a month ago, but I was so angry with him that I did not help him. It is all my fault." Deepa's voice was breaking due to sobbing heavily.

"Don't say all these here. See, Kartik's uncle and aunt have come" Avishek whispered in my ears.

Kartik was from a village far away from Calcutta. His mother died one year ago. In this big city, the only family he had was his uncle and aunt.

The doctor came out from the ICU, and they all were waiting for an answer.

"Who is here from his family?" The doctor asked.

His uncle who was quite shocked showed himself and his aunt.

"I am sorry sir; the boy is in a coma. There are chances he might not wake up. But we all can pray. At this moment only prayer can help us. We are trying our best." The doctor said keeping his eye low.

After hearing this Deepa felt like she was living in a nightmare and she started feeling dizzy, suddenly everything around her became blurred and she collapsed on the ground.

Present Day

"Hey, Are you alright?" Deepa's boyfriend Nikhil came into the room. Nikhil has a tall and slim figure. He had a squared shaped handsome face.

"I want to tell you something," Deepa mumbled.

"I am all ears," Nikhil said and sat on the bed beside Deepa.

"I had a boyfriend," Deepa said while looking down.

"Don't we all have exes?" Nikhil laughed hard.

"He died by committing suicide and I feel guilty that even at the time of his depression I ignored him," Deepa said while tears were falling down her cheeks, she started shivering heavily.

Nikhil remained silent without understanding what to reply.

"I don't think I can do this job anymore and I don't feel I have moved on yet, I don't want to stay with you anymore,"

Deepa said as she wiped her tears.

Nikhil got so angry after listening to this that he didn't even say a single word and went out of the room.

******

After Kartik died Deepa was diagnosed with post-traumatic stress disorder and after years of therapy she felt that she finally had moved on but today seeing that girl in her chamber she felt that nothing had changed and she hadn't been healed. Deepa left her job and her home too after a few days and went to a meditation camp.

Instead of being a visitor at the camp, she started working as a volunteer there. She detached from everyone and worked for almost six months there and then one day a sudden change happened.

One evening everyone was meditating in a closed room. Deepa was also there along with all the visitors. Suddenly a young girl started having breathing difficulties while meditating. Everyone in the room started looking at each other in confusion and panic.

Deepa went close to the young girl and held her hand.

"Take deep breaths through your nostrils with me."

The young girl looked at Deepa and did the same.

"Now exhale through your mouth."

After repeating this a few times, the girl became calm, and she thanked Deepa. Though everyone was confused Deepa understood that it was an anxiety attack and she realized that her real job was helping people who were not able to help themselves.

She thought that once in her life she couldn't help someone but that is giving her the reason to help others. She again came back to her city and started helping people to heal themselves in a way so that she could also get healed from her past traumas.

Author- Suvechha Roy

Suvechha Roy is a Kolkata-based author. Her debut novel was "Heal your wounds with my love". She loves to write about mental health-related topics as she suffered from borderline personality disorder. After struggling for six years with BPD she calls herself a BPD warrior. She writes novels and short stories to create mental health awareness in people. Other than this Suvechha got graduated in mathematics with honours from Presidency University. She has also worked as a school teacher and SAT math faculty.

CHAPTER ELEVEN

Unraveling the Hormone Puzzle

Introducing Tara

Meet Tara, a vibrant 29-year-old Software professional as an educator who seems to have it all together on her platter. She believes in hard work, beneath her confident exterior, Tara struggles with myriads of health issues that have stopped her from dreaming big for years. It doesn't matter to her what other people are saying. Despite her family belonging to be very conservative background, she got an opportunity to learn and to get jobs in top reputed government research organizations. She may not be the topper in school or college but every time she earned satisfactory scores in academics. When it comes to other activities, Tara is an amazing sportsperson who has participated in marathons for social causes starting from her school times. She was also an NCC candidate but couldn't pursue further because her family wanted her to be an IITian. However, she failed in that too. She would have not stopped herself here from what her parents wanted to see as an Engineer, then Assistant Professor she had nailed it anyhow.

Tara's roller-coaster dream

Till now everything was going great with Tara. She got her post-graduation degree. She had fulfilled her parent's dreams. She is now independent with her earnings and she is managing her expenses. She had a childhood dream of getting into the defense and that too in the Air Force Service. But when her parents strictly denied of pursuing this career and asked her to just get married. This was Tara's first turning point of the career. She is not interested in engineering but still took all the entrance exams with the help of coaching. This time was her first lowest point where she was been under pressure of taking the toughest competitive exam in India to get admission into IIT. Here Tara got shrugged off from her desired career and she was satisfied with what her parents wanted. Things eventually got better when she got admission to Engineering college. Starting from day one she was not interested in learning but at the same time, she was scared of getting failed. There are so many students like Tara who are admitted to engineering college but their desire to do something else still resides in their heart. She passed all her semesters with good grades and was placed in an MNC company. Till now she was not happy with the engineering course but the moment she got the offer letter, her emotions were on cloud nine. Finally, the time came when she could earn on her own. She left her home with her father in another city for a job. Since her father was very close to her and protective, he went with Tara to drop her to the girl's hostel. This is the very first time she is going to live away from her family. h Tara's father came back home and cried a lot. He used to miss Tara every single day at home. He was retired and always thinking about Tara's future. Day by day Tara was feeling lonely in a new city. She made some friends and got into a relationship but her dream was soaring she couldn't pay attention to her job and other stuff. In the new city, she struggled to earn more but couldn't. One day Tara's father asked her to pursue higher studies. She came back to her home city and started doing her post-graduation. Once the post-graduation was completed she got her first research job. She was so happy to receive the job but on the other hand, she got worried about her father's health. He was a diabetic patient with a heart problem. Her targeted studies were completed and got a job also. Now after all her roller coaster studies and dreams, she is much more satisfied with her career and earnings. Ready for the new phase of her life to get married.

Symptoms Unveiled

Till now Tara was happy and satisfied for herself. Somewhere in starting off her career or choosing the career she was confused but that was not the part of stress. Why I said the matter of stress because she was diagnosed with one of the hormonal imbalance problems. Healthwise Tara was a very active student in her school and college life but when coming to the professional life where she is earning and happy, she started facing health issues, and that too after Covid-19. She began to feel desperate, depressed, and anxious. During that duration, she lost her father to Covid-19 infection but the rest of her family survived. After this incident, she was not only physically weak but mentally also. There were times when a simple walk left her exhausted and crashed her on the sofa. Since Tara is the elder sibling in the family after her father's death, the family became impatient with her constant fatigue. Wasn't it time she got help for her depression? But she knew she wasn't depressed.

As per medical research about one-third of the people are diagnosed with stress, anxiety, and depression during covid 19 pandemic. From clinical evidence, COVID-19 viral infection affected hormonal imbalance leading to changes in the menstrual cycle. Psychological stress leads to the worsening of symptoms associated with menstruation like thyroid and PCOD.

Tara was detected by the thyroid that had inherited from her father's gene and PCOD due to stress in life. At the initial stage, it is stress or hormonal fluctuations, she soon realizes something more serious might play when the irregularities persist. Besides irregular periods, she struggles with unexplained weight gain, acne breakouts, and debilitating fatigue.

Seeking Answers for Hormonal Imbalance

The thyroid is something she is genetic but PCOD is attached to this thyroid came into the picture after numerous doctor visits and checkups. The news comes as a shock, leaving her feeling overwhelmed and uncertain about her future. Tara was broken up after listening to this. Frustrated and concerned about her future. Like Tara, there are lots of unmarried women who do not openly talk about PCOD especially.

How does PCOD impact daily life?

After the detection of PCOD with thyroid it was a constant battle for Tara to prove she was fine. There were times Tara struggled to manage her weight despite lots of effort and exercise. And after some time of covid 19 lockdown, she reduced 15 kg of weight. At the same time, their emotional nature is haunting her which leads to mood swings and feelings of missing out from societal standards.

Health Empowerment Through Knowledge

When going through many hardships related to career and personal life Tara refuses to let PCOD define her. She went to research, educating herself about the condition and seeking out support online. She had not only consulted the Doctors but also started connecting women who share similar experiences of hormonal imbalance. Just like basic literacy is important in the same way knowing about your own body is important in the long run. Finally, Tara knew the cause of hormonal imbalance and how to overcome it. She used to exercise consistently, eat healthy, and get proper sleep.

A Journey of Self-Discovery

In the struggle with PCOD, Tara embarks on the journey of self-discovery and acceptance in life. She had learned to prioritize self-care, set boundaries to manage stress and practice mindfulness techniques. She had avoided all nonsense talk from people who were acting on her back. Not expecting any help from anyone but believing herself that she could manage till the last breath. PCOD cannot be fully cured but it can be managed through a healthy lifestyle and regular exercise.

Tara finding Hope

It is the harsh reality of PCOD and thyroid which remains a part of Tara's life. Now she is finding hope in small victories along the way. She started achieving a personal fitness milestone, finding peace in creative outlets like journaling or simple embracing moments in nature. Tara had learned to celebrate her resilience and a newfound sense of her happiness. She lives in her childhood memories where she can be happy once again.

At least concluding Tara's story by saying that it is the ongoing journey of hormonal imbalance for PCOD and thyroid. Marked by highs and lows but through it all Tara emerges strong and more resilient. Till now she faced the future with courage and knowing that she is more than her diagnosis.

Author- Tanushree Dholpuria

Tanushree Dholpuria is an Assistant Professor of Computer Science at Engineering College. With a passion for both teaching and writing, Tanushree brings a unique blend of academic and creative work. Outside the classroom, Tanushree is an avid writer, crafting compelling stories and insightful blogs that explore human experiences. Her writing has been featured in blogs, journals and anthologies books that are praised for her vivid imagery and emotional depth. Apart from this Tanushree is also a passionate nature lover and voice behind the podcast "Let's Talk Green". She is connected with nature and shares her views on sustainable living in her podcast episodes. Balancing her professional career and her love for writing, Tanushree Dholpuria continues to inspire both students and readers with her dedication to the written word.

Thank You

Dialogues around mental health are the need of the hour, but talking about it or acknowledging the same is not as easy as it seems to be. "You are not your Mental Health" is a small initiative from WeTalk to start acknowledging the issues through art and storytelling. And it was a surreal experience to see people sharing the same effort in making the anthology book – You Are Not Your Mental Health!

I am very grateful to each and every writer who took the effort and time to contribute to the theme "Mental Health", no matter whether your draft cleared the selection process or not. Your effort and time matter the most.

Thank you, to all the writers who cleared the selection process, it was a privilege reading your drafts.

Thank you, **Dr. Shambhavi Samir Alve**, for the insightful foreword, we couldn't ask for more.

Thank you, **Vinay Kulkarni**, for the last-minute polish and edits.

Thank you, husband, and my four kids (two fur balls included) for giving me much required time and space while making a book.

Last but not least thank you to my elder daughter Anamika, who is the inspiration behind the theme.

To, all the people who shared their thoughts, experiences, and pain (a few stories also mention real-life experiences), thank you from the bottom of my heart. You all are an inspiration!

With love and hugs
Sheeba Vinay